KDN.

Gunsmoke Express

Thanks to a tip-off, Sheriff Alec Lawson and his deputies fight and capture the notorious outlaw Saul York. But the trouble doesn't end there. Alec falls desperately ill and when he recovers, he finds that York's lawyer has got him out on bail. Although still weakened by his illness, Alec is determined to get back to work. He soon finds himself in the action again, but fatigue leads to a terrible mistake and he begins to doubt his abilities. Will his frailty endanger his friends? York is still out there somewhere, protected by his ambitious lawyer.

When York becomes his prime suspect in a murderous robbery, Alec Lawson must push himself to close the net on the elusive outlaw. He'll have to face down a lynch mob, the killer outlaw and his own doubts to get the job done, whatever the cost to himself.

Gunsmoke Express

Gillian F. Taylor

A Black Horse Western

ROBERT HALE

© Gillian F. Taylor 2019
First published in Great Britain 2019

ISBN 978-0-7198-2954-3

The Crowood Press
The Stable Block
Crowood Lane
Ramsbury
Marlborough
Wiltshire SN8 2HR

www.bhwesterns.com

Robert Hale is an imprint
of The Crowood Press

The right of Gillian F. Taylor to be identified as
author of this work has been asserted by her
in accordance with the Copyright, Designs and
Patents Act 1988

Typeset by
Derek Doyle & Associates, Shaw Heath
Printed and bound in Great Britain by
4Bind Ltd, Stevenage, SG1 2XT

Dedicated to Ian Liston,
who was delighted at being Sam.

CHAPTER ONE

The four horsemen headed up the gulch at a steady pace. They kept together with the skill of well-drilled cavalrymen, no one getting ahead or behind. The horses' glossy coats were darkened with the sweat of a Colorado summer but all four travelled well, ears pricked and alert to their riders' commands. The lead rider, Sheriff Alec Lawson, signalled to his deputies. All four dropped smoothly into a walk, acting together with the same precision. The horses stretched their necks, snorted and let out gusty breaths as they relaxed after their long, fast journey. The men relaxed too. The sheriff shifted in his saddle, wincing slightly as he eased his right leg.

'Are you all right, Alec?' asked Karl Firth, his senior deputy.

'Aye.' Alec Lawson's Scottish roots were clear even in just that word. 'I'll be fine for what we hafta do.' The sentence ended with a cough, but he paid no more attention to that than he did to the ache in his thigh, the legacy of a bullet wound received a couple of months earlier. Alec wasn't yet fully recovered from the injury, but he had got bored of spending most of his time in the office. A tip-off to the hideout of an outlaw gang had been just the excuse he needed to get back into the saddle and out into the wild country he loved.

These were the foothills of the great Rocky Mountains, rolling land with dry, mostly scrubby vegetation. Bigger trees clustered along the sides of the gulch, and in patches along the tumbling creek. Not far ahead, a scrap of open land showed the scars where someone had been searching for gold the previous year.

'Boss, I know this place.' Sam Liston spoke up, his accent a pleasant, Kentucky drawl.

Alec halted his sandy dun horse, turning to his friend.

'This was where those two miners got into a fight over the best way to cook eggs and it ended with one of them smacking the other in the head with a pan full of eggs and hot fat.' Sam's handsome, boyish face was alight with merriment.

8

'I remember,' said Ethan, shaking his head sadly. 'A shameful waste of good eggs, it was.' His long face was mournful, but that was his natural expression. While Sam was habitually the clown of the party, Ethan tended to be pessimistic. In both cases, it was an exaggeration of a natural trait, to lighten the mood of their demanding work.

'It's sure funny how gold fever takes some folk,' Sam said. 'I recall a feller once, who. . . .'

'Do ye recall whereabouts the dugout is in this gulch?' Alec interrupted. 'If it ain't too much trouble to ask ye tae do yer job,' he added in a mild tone that didn't match his firm expression.

Sam smiled, unabashed. 'Since you asked so polite and all. . . .' He dropped the humour, becoming fully professional as he described the land ahead. 'Just after those willows, the gulch curves to the left. It opens up some, then narrows to a V going up the head of the valley. The dugout's in the slope to the right of the V, so it faces south, for the light. The door's made of logs and there's a couple of windows to the right. I think one was greased paper, but I'm not sure.'

'What about cover?' Alec asked.

'Not much once you get past the trees. We'd best to leave the horses there,' Sam answered. 'There's some willow and shrub along of the creek

9

but I reckon it's crawling most of the way to get close without being seen.'

'If both the windows are greased paper, that'll make things easier,' Karl said.

Greased paper windows were not uncommon in dugouts and other temporary buildings like shacks. They served to keep out insects, snakes and rodents, while still allowing in a little light, and had the great advantage of being cheap.

'They've probably got the door open for extra light,' Alec pointed out. 'We'll go take a look. No chatter, we don't want them to hear us coming.' He nudged his horse into a walk and led the way.

They tethered their horses just inside the shade of the trees, watering them and loosening their girths. Moving carefully, the lawmen worked their way through the trees and shrubs. Alec limped, but made no more noise than the others. At the other side of the copse, they crouched behind a tangle of thimbleberry bushes and some young chokecherry trees that clustered among the willows. The head of the gulch was as Sam had described it. The dugout was set back into the slope of the surrounding hills. The dirt-covered roof was almost indistinguishable from the surrounding ground, with grasses growing on it. A tin stove chimney stuck up incongruously, and thin smoke drifted upwards. The wooden front was already weathered and softened, but still looked unnatural in the otherwise natural setting. As Alec had guessed, the door was open but they couldn't see what was happening inside. Seven horses were picketed on a line on the other side of the open space.

'Looks like someone's at home,' Karl said softly.

'And unless a couple of those are packhorses, there's more'n five of them,' Ethan added. 'I done told you that tip-off wasn't straight.'

'We were outnumbered anyway, what difference does a couple more make?' Alec asked, flashing a quick glance at his friends. His brown eyes were bright with a spark of recklessness that sobered as he turned to study the ground.

'Why'd they have to be holed up inside?' Sam said. 'It's got to be as dark as the inside of a cow's belly in there. It'd make our job easier if'n they came outside and played cards in the light, like civilized folk.'

As if an answer to his complaint, they suddenly heard a woman's laugh, and a burst of cheers from the dugout.

'I guess we know why they're inside,' Karl said drily.

There was some more laughing and whooping from the outlaw hideout.

'Damned if'n I didn't take up the wrong profession,' Sam said. 'I know I'd rather be playing strip poker than trying to figure out how to get a bunch of outlaws out of a dugout.'

Ethan was about to give his opinion on Sam's poker skills when Alec signalled him to stay quiet.

'Has anyone got a clean handkerchief?' Alec asked, stifling a cough.

Karl produced one and handed it over. 'I was raised to always carry one,' he remarked drily.

'So was I, but mine's worn thin in the centre,' Alec answered evenly. 'Sam, go fetch my powder horn from my saddle-bag, please.' He held up Karl's fine cotton handkerchief and inspected it, as Karl watched suspiciously.

Sam was soon back with the powder horn. It was a handsome one, given to Alec by the men of his company when he retired from the 5th Cavalry. Somehow they'd found a Scottish one, with silver fittings embellished with a thistle design, and a topaz on the stopper. Of course, Alec used metal cartridges in his guns and didn't need loose gunpowder, but he was fond of the powder horn, and often kept it in his saddle bag, in spite of occasional teasing from his friends.

'I've been telling you there'll be a need for this some time,' he said, taking it from Sam. Alec laid

Karl's handkerchief on the ground and poured a small mound of gunpowder into the centre. Picking the handkerchief up, he wrapped the fine fabric tightly around the gunpowder, twisted it, and kept wrapping and twisting until he had a hard little ball knotted together. 'A wee bomb.' He held it out to display it.

'I'm not lending you a handkerchief ever again,' Karl said.

Alec's chuckle broke off into a cough. 'I told ye mine was too worn tae make a good seal,' he said when he'd recovered. 'I reckon this is packed tight enough to make a nice bang and scare the outlaws out of their bolthole.'

'Are you planning to throw it in through the door?' Ethan asked.

Alec shook his head. 'There's just about enough cover for someone to sneak around and get up on the roof. They drop this down the chimney; when it hits the fire – boom!'

Karl glanced through the bushes at the dugout. 'If someone's going to be walking around on that roof, it'll have to be the lightest of us. Which is you, Alec.'

Alec stared at him for a moment, before shrugging to acknowledge the truth. He and Sam were the same height, both a little below average, but while Sam was broad-shouldered and well built, Alec was lithe and slender. His active life meant he was stronger than he looked, but he sometimes felt he was rather unimposing compared to his deputies. Tucking the improvised bomb into the pocket of his brown jacket, Alec issued orders to his men. After wishing them good luck, he began his cautious approach to the dugout.

Getting to the roof of the dugout unseen meant slow and careful movement. Alec had a well-honed eye for the land and excellent spatial awareness, which enabled him to find hollows and features that hid him from the outlaws' position. The possibility of being spotted brought sharpness to his nerves that he welcomed after the weeks of enforced idleness. Alec was unaware that he was smiling as he safely drew level with the front of the dugout, and picked his way up the rise of the hill. Only when he reached the flat area of the concealed roof did he pause to catch his breath.

As he waited for the slight pain in his chest to ease, Alec looked out into the gulch below. He knew roughly where his friends were, but couldn't make them out. Satisfied that all was as well as it could be, Alec began the delicate task of crawling across to the chimney. Although the top of the dugout looked as solid as the slope it was built into, the roof was made of layers of interwoven branches topped with soil. Alec's caution was wise; he was almost within reach of the chimney when he felt the roof sag beneath his right hand as he crawled. Dried branches beneath the layer of soil creaked audibly, not doubt sending some fine dirt down into the room below. Quickly shifting his weight to his left side, Alec paused to recover his balance and listen. There were no cries of outrage or warning from inside the dugout, just indistinguishable talk and some laughter. Once steady, he moved again, changing direction slightly and testing the ground carefully with each hand before putting weight on it. A few slow moves later and he was beside the chimney.

Alec fetched the improvized bomb from his pocket, and slipped a cartridge from his gunbelt as an added surprise. Suppressing a grin, he dropped the bomb into the chimney, and the cartridge a moment later. Shuffling backwards quickly, he was barely three feet away when there was a muffled bang from below and a cloud of soot spurted from the mouth of the chimney. A split second later there was the crack of a shot. There were startled shouts and a piercing scream from a woman; for a moment, Alec thought the bullet might have exploded from the stove and injured someone.

There was a sudden commotion below as people came running out of the dugout in confusion. Two of the men and one of the women were only partially dressed, the woman's long, unnaturally red hair blowing loose in tangled strands. Six people altogether came into Alec's view, though he couldn't see any close to the front of the dugout from his position on the top. As they paused to mill about, shouting questions to one another, Alec's three deputies burst out from their places in the trees.

'Surrender! You're all under arrest!' Karl's order was loud and clear.

Chaos broke out. Two men snatched out guns and started to fire. One man and one of the women threw themselves flat on the ground. One man raced towards the picketed horses. The red-haired woman spun and headed back to the dugout. Alec's deputies returned fire, their guns adding to the confusion and noise. Watching everything from his place on the roof, Alec was pretty certain that he'd not yet seen Saul York, the leader of the outlaws. Anxious to know where York was, Alec half rose, drew his revolver, and started forwards on a diagonal path to the front of the dugout.

On his second step, the roof gave way beneath

him. Dry branches cracked with a sound like gun-shots, the ends scraping him and snagging in his clothes as he tumbled down through the hole. Alec tried grabbing something with his free hand but there were only small clumps of grass, which tore loose. Tumbling into the unknown amid a shower of dirt, Alec felt his legs strike something even as his head was scraping through the hole. Whatever he struck moved and collapsed beneath him. Alec hit the ground on top of another person – a man, from the grunt of pain. He was thrown off by his momentum, losing his grip on his revolver. It clattered away into the surrounding shadows. Alec barely noticed. His lungs seemed full of the fine dirt, racking him with coughs that tore at a chest already stinging from the scrapes inflicted by the branches he'd fallen through. Fortunately, his accidental cushion had been winded by Alec's fall, and wasn't yet capable of acting.

Choking back another cough, Alec struggled to hands and knees and got his first look at whom he'd landed on. With the dim light and circulating dust it was difficult to see much clearly but a shaft of sunlight came through the hole he'd made and illuminated the figure beside him. It was a man of average height and build, with light brown hair and smallpox scars scattered over his face. Most distinctive were the bright blue eyes, disconcertingly like Karl's in colour, but colder in emotion. As he registered that it was Saul York, Alec glanced about for his gun. Spotting the revolver, he dived towards it.

His hand was almost on it when he was grabbed from behind. Alec was pulled onto his back and kept rolling towards York, partially freeing himself from the other man's grip. As York tried to seize his left arm, Alec used the momentum of his roll to launch a kick. He was too close to get much power into it but York grunted with pain. It didn't slow him, though. Holding Alec firmly, York twisted, pulling Alec clear over himself and pushing him away. Alec rolled helplessly across the dirt floor and fetched up hard against a wooden bench. Pain shot through his chest as he gasped at the impact and began coughing.

For a few moments, Alec could do little more than fight for breath. He managed to turn onto his side so he could see York. The outlaw was on hands and knees, looking about. Alec saw his gaze settle on something. He looked, and saw a gunbelt hanging on the back of a chair. As York started forward, Alec forced himself up and lunged forward in a desperate tackle. He threw himself against the outlaw hard enough to knock him over and send the two of them sprawling on the floor again in a tangle of arms and legs. Alec's chest was still heaving as he fought for each painful breath. His right arm was pinned beneath himself and York grabbed his left arm before Alec could respond. Alec felt his strength ebbing and knew he had to act quickly. He had to fight in whatever way he could, or die. As another cough rose, he gathered himself and spat a gob of phlegm, saliva and dirt into York's eye. York reflexively released Alec's arm to wipe his eye. Alec lashed out instantly, ramming the heel of his hand into the underside of York's chin. York's head snapped backwards, with a stifled noise that had to mean he'd bitten his tongue. The back of his head hit the floor hard. Alec rapidly untangled himself, delivering a punch into the pit of York's stomach as he did so. As York moaned and thrashed about, Alec launched himself across the floor to his gun. Snatching up the short-barrelled Colt, he spun himself around and into a sitting position. York was just sitting up. Alec thumbed back the hammer, using both hands to hold the gun steady.

'Surrender!' The end of the order was strangled as Alec fought back a cough.

York stared back at him, considering, then smiled calmly and raised his hands. Alec was forcing himself to breathe shallowly to ease the pain in his chest, though he still felt breathless after the tussle. His concentration never wavered as he watched the outlaw. Seconds ticked by. Alec didn't dare try to stand until more of his strength returned, but the breathlessness and increasing urge to cough were weakening him. York studied him, waiting.

Alec cleared his throat. 'You can't get away. Ma deputies are outside.'

The sound of gunfire had ceased now.

York smiled. 'Oh, there's no point in just killing you,' he said. 'I doubt if'n I could kill all your deputies too. But they'd let me go if I had you as a hostage. I just got to wait until you start coughing, or that gun gets too heavy and your hands start shaking. . . .' He let the threat trail off.

Alec smiled in return, a thin, dangerous smile. 'That's going tae be a long wait,' he said, with far more confidence than he actually felt.

CHAPTER TWO

The light from the doorway dimmed.

'You never could stay away from the action, Alec,' said Karl Firth. He moved into Alec's line of sight, his gun also trained on York. Behind him was Sam, who grinned at Alec.

'You all look like you done fought a wildcat and lost,' he remarked.

Alec lowered his gun thankfully as his deputies cuffed York efficiently. Karl looked very nearly as composed and tidy as when they'd left Lucasville earlier. Light clouds of dirt cascaded off Alec as he pulled himself slowly to his feet. He straightened his rumpled clothing, discovering a rent in the sleeve of his jacket, and pulled some dry vegetation from his tousled hair before putting on the hat that Sam handed him.

Outside, Alec limped over to the creek to tidy up properly and refresh himself, while his deputies sorted out the prisoners. One of the outlaws was dead and another was moaning persistently, clutching a belly wound. The other two men and the prostitutes had surrendered quickly. The injured man's wound was tended as best they could manage. York waited next to the women, chatting to them and ignoring what was happening as though it didn't concern him. When Sam went to collect the lawmen's horses, Alec got to his feet and went to join the others. Karl explained what he'd planned.

'Sam's going to ride ahead and get back to Lyons first to arrange for a buckboard. He'll come back and collect the dead fellow there, and Robbins. The rest of us will escort the uninjured back to town, leave the women there, and get York, Patterson and Farlow to the county jail. Sam will follow with the buckboard.'

'That sounds reasonable,' Alec replied. He glanced over at York and saw him pressing himself against the red-haired woman, who backed away. York laughed at her discomfort. Alec looked at him with a feeling of distaste. 'Let's get this lot mounted and away.'

He stalked over to York, doing his best to

conceal his limp. 'Come on. You're on that bay.' Alec pointed to the horse he meant.

York shook his head. 'That ain't my horse. Mine's the sorrel; I'm riding my horse.' He stated it as a fact.

'You ride the bay, or you walk tae the jail on your own feet with a rope around your neck.' Alec's answer was calm but firm. 'Make more of a fuss and you'll be riding in the buckboard just like Robbins,' he pointed to the injured man.

York heaved a sigh of irritation, but did as he was told.

Alec let himself in through the rear door of the sheriff's building, where all four of them lived and worked. Lobbing his hat onto the table at the kitchen end of the room, he ran his fingers through his dishevelled hair, limped to his armchair, and collapsed into it gratefully. Leaning his head against the high back of the chair, he was grateful to be inside, out of the mid-afternoon sun. This room was the rear half of the ground floor: the front half was divided into a large office, where his deputies worked, and a smaller one that was Alec's.

All these rooms were functional rather than cosy. The kitchen area had a cook stove, cupboards, a plain table and chairs. The living area

was a little more personal. There were four comfortable chairs gathered around a small heating
stove, with a couple of small tables for mugs and
books. Karl's chair was red leather and looked as
though it belonged in a gentleman's club; Alec
thought it was just right for his aristocratic-looking
friend. Sam's chair was covered with flowered
chintz that looked incongruous in the otherwise
masculine surroundings. Ethan's chair was a plain,
wooden rocker, softened with a patchwork com-
forter. His own chair had a high wingback, which
he liked for keeping draughts off, and because he
could rest his head against it. There was also a
rather handsome walnut sideboard, beautifully
polished, that Karl had inherited. Above it were
plain wooden shelves sporting a few books, a
checkers set, a comb belonging to Sam and a silver
trophy that Alec had won in a horse-riding compe-
tition in the army.

Alec let his eyes close, but any attempt at rest was
interrupted by the sound of feet coming down the
stairs at the rear of the room. He lifted his head
from the back of the chair to look round as Mrs
Andersen entered, carrying a cloth bag full of
laundry. Her round, kindly face broke into a smile
as she saw him.

'You are home already, Sheriff Alec. I saw dere

was no one here, and Mr Beyer, he say you were all gone to catch a bad man.'

The housekeeper was a middle-aged Swedish widow. Her flaxen hair was in a thick braid wound round her head like a crown, lending dignity to her comfortable appearance. With her husband dead for over a year, and her two sons in the army, she enjoyed looking after the four lawmen and they enjoyed not needing to worry about house-keeping after long, active days at work.

'That's right,' Alec agreed. Beyer was their sta-bleman, who looked after the half dozen horses belonging to the law office. 'We got a tip-off about where York was. . . .' His explanation trailed off into a cough. Alec fought it down, trying to ease the pain in his chest it caused. He must have scraped himself worse than he thought during his fall through the roof.

Mrs Andersen set down the bag of laundry and hurried to fetch a glass of water. As she brought it to him, Alec had managed to regain control of his breathing. He smiled his thanks and drank in careful swallows.

'You have done too much,' Mrs Andersen admonished him anxiously. 'You may pay a big price to chase dis man.'

'It was worth it,' Alec replied. 'Saul York isn't just

a bandit, he's vicious. Last spring he was robbing a stagecoach. The guard said he didna have the key tae the strongbox; York didn't believe him. He pistol-whipped the guard and searched him. When the guard didna have the key after all, York blamed him for it, and shot him.' Alec took a sip of the water before continuing. 'In the fall, a madam up in Pinewood Springs complained about how he treated her girls. He said it was his right to do as he liked with them. York beat Foxtail Mary black and blue and then. . . .' Alec made a vague gesture. 'He went back a couple of weeks later and laughed in her face before using a girl badly and walking out without paying. Foxtail Mary sold up and left a week later. It's well worth a few bumps and bruises tae get him behind bars.'

Mrs Andersen nodded. 'You are a good man. But you are also tired; I will make you some food.' She looked towards the door. 'Will the others be here soon?'

Alec shook his head. 'We killed one bandit an' injured another, so Sam's bringing them back to town in a buckboard. Karl and Ethan are taking the others to the jail.'

Mrs Andersen started for the stove, then turned and looked at Alec sternly. 'Why are you not taking dem to the jail?'

Alec had hoped she wouldn't think to ask. However, he didn't want to lie to her. 'I fell through the roof of the dugout, and the ride took more out of me than I expected, so I left ma horse with Sam and came back from Lyons on the train,' he admitted. 'I just need tae rest and eat, and I'll be as good as common.'

She studied him with the wary eye of an experienced mother, then her face softened into an indulgent smile. 'You please rest, Sheriff Alec. I will get you some food.'

'Thank you,' Alec smiled back, and relaxed back into the chair.

Unusually, Alec was the last one down to breakfast in the morning. He only ate some toast and sipped half-heartedly at his coffee.

'You should go back to bed,' Karl told him. 'I spent two months acting as sheriff while you were off playing outlaw with Alcott, if you remember?' In his other role as a deputy state marshal, Alec had posed as an outlaw to bring about the capture of Tom Alcott and his gang. It had ended in gunfire, with the outlaws dead and Alec injured.

'I've spent enough time in bed recently,' Alec insisted, swallowing another cough. It seemed that almost every breath hurt. His stubbornness fought

27

with his honesty. 'I'll no' do much today,' he compromised. 'I'll stay here and start on the paperwork for York and sort the mail. A team of mules were reported stolen from Golden yesterday, two ranchers on the North Saint Vrain are arguing over a boundary, and equipment was stolen from the Little Rose Mine a couple of days back. I'll look over the details and decide who's going where.' He paused, trying to catch his breath without it hurting too much, and became aware of a mild headache. It didn't improve his mood. 'I can still make myself useful.'

Karl looked at the other deputies. 'He looks a little flushed.'

'If he falls over, Mrs Andersen will put him to bed,' Sam said cheerfully.

'It's not fair,' Ethan complained. 'I'd like to go back to bed but you always insist I have to be up during the day. Can you breathe on me, Alec, so I can catch what you've got and go back to bed?' He leaned across the table.

Alec laughed. 'Ow! That hurts.' He forced himself to breathe shallowly. 'I scraped my ribs on the way through the dugout roof,' he explained.

Karl looked at him unconvinced, and then started issuing brisk orders to the other two. Alec shot him a grateful look then sipped his coffee again, relishing the last chance to relax before going to make a start on the day's paperwork.

By the evening, even Alec was willing to admit that he was unwell. He forced down a little of his fried pork and potatoes, refusing coffee in favour of water. Feeling hot, achy and weak, he climbed upstairs and fell gratefully into his bed. By the morning he was feverish, his skin hot and dry. With a headache, and pain in his chest with every dry cough, Alec had no will to protest when Mrs Andersen insisted on sending for the doctor.

He mumbled a couple of answers to the doctor during the examination but it was easier to let Mrs Andersen do most of the talking. Alec simply lay quietly, covered with just a couple of sheets, breathing shallowly to minimize the discomfort. He heard the doctor say pneumonia, but other than passing regret at being faced with more illness and recovery, it didn't mean too much to him. When the doctor left, he sipped some water then fell into a restless doze, punctuated by dry coughs and the frustrating pain that wouldn't let him breathe properly.

As Alec's fever progressed, Mrs Andersen spent more and more time in his hot, shaded room. His friends carried on their work diligently, but would pop up to his room when they had a few minutes. Sam came in quietly on the fourth afternoon, his normally merry face unusually sober as he looked at his friend.

'How is he now?' he asked softly, sitting on the opposite side of the bed to the housekeeper. The drawn curtains kept the sun out of the room but even in the lower light he could see that Alec's face was flushed. Now, when he coughed, Alec brought up rusty-coloured sputum. At the moment, he seemed to be asleep; he didn't open his eyes or respond to Sam's voice. His breathing was still shallow and faster than normal.

'Not good,' Mrs Andersen answered. 'He is too hot and not comfortable.' She leaned forward and brushed his dark hair gently away from his face. '*Mitt barn,*' she murmured.

Alec turned his head slightly towards her, though his eyes stayed closed.

'Ma?' His voice was dry and rough. 'Ma?' It was weaker the second time.

'Shh, *mitt olyckligt barn.*' Mrs Andersen dipped a cloth in a bowl of water, wrung it out, and wiped Alec's face and hands to cool him.

Sam was puzzled for a moment by Alec's response, then remembered something. 'Bairn. It's a Scottish word for child; I've heard him use it now and again,' he said. 'What you said sounded like that; he must have thought you were calling him your child.'

Mrs Andersen glanced at him. 'I was,' she said simply before turning her attention back to Alec. She soaked the cloth again and squeezed water from it into his mouth. Alec swallowed, his eyes half opening for a moment as he took more liquid, before closing again. Mrs Andersen stroked his hair, soothing him as she would her own sons, until he slipped into a deeper sleep. Sitting back in her chair, she watched him for a minute before looking across to Sam.

'He is so sick. We should write his parents; they should know that he may need them. I would want to see my sons if they were sick like this.'

Sam shook his head slowly. 'His ma and pa were killed in a fire when he was fifteen. It happened at night: Alec escaped through a window at the back, but the smoke got to his parents too quick. They likely never woke up. He had some family back in Scotland, but addresses and such got burned up in the fire. He's got no family now.'

'So sad, to be alone.' Mrs Andersen sighed.

'He's got us, his friends,' Sam said with simple sincerity. 'Me and Alec met fourteen years back, when we were new recruits. We were bunkies, both just regular enlisted men. But it was easy to see there was something special about Alec: he was

31

good at what he did and somehow those around him became better at what they did. You knew he would never let you down, and you never wanted to let him down.'

Mrs Andersen looked thoughtfully at Alec. In his exhausted sleep, he looked too frail and vulnerable to be the leader she knew he was. He was more handsome than he realized; his fine, regular features were boyish, but saved from prettiness by the strong, straight brows and arched nose. His large, dark eyes often betrayed his inner strength and experience; he was a man who had both seen and caused death. At the moment, though, he looked to her like a sick child who needed love. She brushed her fingers lightly over his hair once more.

'I pray he will get better.'

'He will,' Sam said with confidence. 'Alec's as stubborn as a mule. If'n he don't want to die, he damn well won't, not from something so ordinary as pneumonia.'

Mrs Andersen smiled at him, and nodded.

Alec burned with fever for another four days before it reached its crisis. At last his temperature dropped and his breathing slowed to normal. The air of quiet tension in the law building lifted and there was laughter and a general sense of relaxation. As weak as he was, Alec was content to remain in his bed and be nursed for a week before demanding to be allowed to get up.

'I want tae move about,' he insisted. 'To see something other than these walls. I'm cut off up here.'

Mrs Andersen knew when to give in. She fetched the clothes he asked for but couldn't stop herself from telling him to take things slowly. Alec barely heard her, pleased at getting his hands on regular clothing again after so long in nightshirts. As soon as she left the room, he slid out of bed and began dressing.

Once downstairs, Alec paused to look around the living quarters, relishing the signs of daily life, like the book on Sam's chair with a dog-eared playing card for a bookmark. He was out to the stable very soon, where the horses not being used were resting away from the sun and flies. Alec always found the company of the horses soothing, and even the familiar smells of horse, straw, leather and muck seemed almost homelike. The visit had to be short, though, as Alec found himself shaky after just a few minutes, and had to return to the house.

As he sat back into his armchair, Karl came through from the front office. His aristocratic face lost its usual reserve as he smiled with pleasure at seeing his friend.

'It's good to see you down here, especially since I bet that you'd bully Mrs Andersen into letting you up today.'

Alec narrowed his eyes. 'So what did the others bet?'

'Sam put his money on yesterday, but Ethan said it would be another couple of days, Thursday, I think.'

Alec rose. 'I reckon I'll go back to bed now and get up tomorrow, so no one makes money out of me. I know Sam and Ethan aren't around, because their horses aren't in the stable. If you say I got up today, I'll just deny it, and I'm the sheriff here.'

Karl scowled at him. 'You're a mean boss, Alec.' There was a pause as they stared at one another, then Karl was the first to smile and laugh.

Alec laughed too. 'It's good tae be here. What were you doin' today? I didn't get a chance tae ask earlier.' In the last week, Karl had been updating Alec regularly on what had happened during his illness. This morning, he'd only made a brief appearance in Alec's room. His relaxed expression changed as Alec spoke. It was subtle, but Alec knew him well. 'What is it?' he demanded.

Karl looked straight at him, regret in his crystal blue eyes. 'York's not behind bars, Alec. He's out and free.'

CHAPTER THREE

'What?' exclaimed Alec. 'York's free?'

'No.' Karl shook his head. 'I'm sorry, I didn't explain that well. He's out on bail.'

Alec frowned. 'Bail? How'd he get bail? What was it set at?'

'Judge Linford set it at a thousand dollars. York's attorney stood the money for him.'

'That's a lot to risk on a no-good like York,' Alec said. 'Who's his attorney?'

'Name's Bob Hart.' Seeing Alec's puzzled look, Karl explained. 'He came to Lucasville and set up back in about March, while you were away with Alcott.'

Alec considered. 'What do ye make of this Hart?'

'An up and coming sort,' Karl told him. 'Dresses

real smart, well spoken. He gives out that he's going to be the biggest law wrangler in town someday, and how he's already got a fair deal of money. York's the biggest case he's taken since he's been here.'

Alec frowned. 'York's got tae have an attorney, but why is Hart taking him on? He doesna' sound like someone who'd be interested in taking on a dirty job like that.'

'I'm guessing he reckons a big case like this could make his name.'

'Only if he wins it and York goes free, and if York skips bail then that's a thousand dollars Hart won't see again.'

Karl shrugged. 'Like I said, Hart's ambitious and willing to take the risk.'

Alec nodded. 'Thanks. I'll call on him and get a feel for him myself.'

Karl smiled. 'Not today, though. You're not going to impress anyone if you collapse in the middle of the conversation. And besides, maybe you should check in the mirror before you go visiting.'

Alec ran his hand over his bristly jaw. Mrs Andersen had kept his whiskers trimmed short while he was too ill to shave, but he needed to visit the barber to get back to being properly clean-shaven, as he preferred. What's more, he realized, his hair needed cutting too. Alec's one vanity was his thick, dark hair. Since leaving the military, he'd taken the opportunity to wear it at almost collar length, but now it was decidedly untidy.

'Aye, well. Mebbe tomorrow,' he said. 'I want things tae be back tae normal again. I feel like I've missed so much this year; it's the summer now.'

'And speaking of missing things, I've got to ask around and see if I can find out anything about some stolen liquor,' Karl said. 'If I get a hustle on, I should be able to make it out to Lyons and back today.' He stood up. 'It's good to see you back on your feet again, Alec.'

'I'm looking forward to getting back in the saddle again,' Alec replied, smiling.

In spite of his optimism, Alec found he still tired quickly. In the next couple of days, he just pottered about the stables and strolled to the end of the block and back, before sitting on a bench and just relishing the sunshine on his skin. He took possession of his office again, catching up on reports on what had happened during his illness. He found his weakness frustrating but there was some consolation in that the enforced rest had done his leg good, and there was little trace of a limp.

The third day after getting up, Alec set off for the barber's determinedly. Passing through the busy town, seeing the hustle and bustle and hearing the chatter of other voices, his mood lightened. It felt as though he were returning to life again. Once shaved and barbered, Alec walked home with something of his usual briskness. He had intended to rest on his bed, but decided to visit his horse instead.

In the pleasant shade of Biscuit's box stall, his horse turned to him, blowing gently through its nostrils in greeting. Alec patted his creamy brown neck and then delicately touched the soft velvet of the horse's muzzle. Biscuit's kind, dark eyes gleamed in the low light as the horse nuzzled Alec's hand. Alec rested one arm across his horse's back and leaned against him, stroking him steadily with his free hand. The horse's head lowered as he relaxed, one ear flickering back towards his owner now and again.

Standing here with his horse, Alec also knew how much being able to ride out into the wild country mattered to him. It gave him a sense of being able to breathe freely, which he never really felt in a town. As fulfilling as his job was, Alec's dream was to one day have a horse ranch. The ranch wouldn't just be work, it would be home too: a family home where he would be with his wife and children. For a long time, the wife had been a faceless figure, just a presence that he needed to complete the picture. Now, at last, Alec felt that the figure had a face and a name.

'The men that sold her were scum,' he told the patient horse, who cocked an ear back to his voice. 'But one of them did something beautiful when he called her Lily.'

Alec smiled as he thought of the young Chinese woman he'd rescued from slavery the year before. He'd placed her in the care of the Reverend Brown, whose wife had enthusiastically adopted the girl as a daughter. Lily had been taught to read, write and do sums, and to cook, sew and run a household.

'She's as lovely as any hothouse flower,' Alec told his horse. 'She's exotic, like a rare bird that just visits for the winter.'

'Are y'all talking to your horse again?'

Sam's cheerful drawl startled Alec. He looked round to see Sam leading his pretty paint mare into the stable. 'At least Biscuit's better at conversation than you,' Alec retorted.

Sam adopted a hurt expression. 'I'm going to overlook your wounding remark on the grounds that your brain got addled some on account of the fever you had recent.'

Alec grinned fiercely. 'If you reckon I'm addled,

then how about a game of cribbage this evening? After all, you're sure and certain to win, so why not have a bet on it?'

'Because it's not my brain that's addled, and I know better than to bet against you at cribbage, no matter what state you're in.'

'I don't see why being in Colorado should make a difference to how I play cribbage.'

Sam snatched his hat off and threw it at Alec, who caught it handily. In the same move, Alec dropped it on his own head, but as it was too large, it slipped down over his eyes. Both of them burst out laughing.

'Here.' Alec tossed the hat back. 'I'd best get back to the office.'

Sam slapped it on his head with a flourish. 'I'll see Calico's settled, then fix some coffee. Not that you deserve any,' he added.

Alec grinned. 'Doesn't matter whether I deserve it, I'm in charge of the wages.'

Sam sighed, and led his horse on. 'I think I preferred it when Karl was in charge,' he grumbled.

Patting his horse farewell, Alec left the stable, whistling cheerfully.

'Mr Hart will see you,' the secretary said.

'Thank you,' Alec replied, smiling politely at the

young lady.

She smiled back, colouring slightly and looking bashful as she returned to her desk. Alec was a little puzzled by her flustered movements as she seated herself, but assumed that perhaps she was new in the job and uncertain. After all, he'd been surprised himself on finding that Hart's secretary was a pretty, young woman but then there seemed to be a lot that was new and modern about the lawyer's premises. The furniture all looked new, and there was a typewriter on the desk, something Alec had only seen a couple of times before. Much as he'd have liked to stop and examine it, he went through into the main office where Hart was waiting.

'Good morning, Sheriff Lawson. It's a pleasure to meet you.' Bob Hart rose and came around his gleaming, leather-topped desk to offer his hand. The lawyer was much taller than Alec, and a few years younger, with the build of a powerful athlete under his well-cut suit. He had short, curling blond hair and was decidedly handsome with a noble profile. Altogether, he reminded Alec of pictures of ancient Greek statues he'd seen in a schoolbook.

They shook hands, and Hart gestured to a silver tray holding decanters and glasses, on a table at the side of the room. 'Would you care for a drink?'

'I wouldn't usually, but this isna' a formal visit
. . . so I'll tek a whiskey, thank you.'

Hart poured a generous portion into a cut-glass
tumbler and handed it to Alec, before pouring
himself a brandy and sitting down. Alec swirled his
glass lightly, sniffed the liquor, and then took a sip.
He let it pool on his tongue a few moments,
savouring the smoky richness, before swallowing.

'That's a fine whiskey,' he said approvingly.

'Yes, it's one of the best,' Hart agreed. 'Of
course, wine spirits are superior to grain spirits.'
He held up his glass of brandy. 'And brandy is the
finest of them all. It's a gentleman's drink, but I
keep whiskey for guests who prefer it.'

'Of course,' Alec agreed mildly, somewhat
amused by the way Hart's self-confidence in his
belief meant that he didn't notice the implied
insult to his current guest's tastes. Glancing about
the office, he saw two or three gold-framed certifi-
cates, including Hart's law qualifications. There was
also a framed photo of the Lucasville City Council,
with Hart clearly visible in the middle of the group.

'I was voted onto the council last month,' Hart
said proudly.

'You have time to be on the council as well as
your law work?' Alec asked, taking another sip of
whiskey.

'It isn't always easy,' Hart said. 'But I want to contribute to this town. It's a way of making acquaintances here and earning myself a place.'

'And publicizing your name.'

'All the council members are public figures and some of the others are businessmen too. If I just wanted easy publicity I could put an advertisement in the *Lucasville Trumpet*. Running a town is work.'

Alec nodded agreement, while privately reflecting that it was also work that put Hart in touch with some of the most influential and prosperous men in town. He decided to get to the point of his visit.

'I understand that you're representing Saul York,' he said. 'I would ha' thought him a risky case to take on.'

Hart smiled. 'You're a lawman, Sheriff Lawson. Your work is also about risk, and at least mine isn't likely to get me shot.'

'I guess you've no' been west very long,' Alec replied dryly. 'I known lawyers who disagreed with their clients and got shot.'

Hart only hesitated briefly. 'Well, I don't expect to lose enough cases for that to be much of a risk.' He gestured around the room. 'You don't earn a set-up like this by losing cases.'

'I guess not. You know York's a killer?'

'He's *accused* of being a killer,' Hart pointed out.

43

'It hasn't been proven yet, so calling him a killer is slander.'

Alec grunted. 'I saw myself what he did to Foxtail Mary. He deserves prison for that.'

'My client denies ever meeting her, and it's his word against a whore's. There's not a jury that would take the word of any woman, let alone a common, filthy whore, over a man's, even if she did testify.' Hart radiated self-assurance.

Alec gritted his teeth in frustration, knowing that Hart was correct. 'Did York ask for you, or did you volunteer to defend him?' he asked.

'I heard about his case and offered my services. No public defender could get him acquitted, so he needed me, and I want to make my mark here, so I needed his case to defend. It's a winning situation for both of us.' Hart smiled and sampled his brandy.

Alec also took a drink, giving himself time to think. 'York has been on the wanted lists for three or four years. Getting him acquitted for all the charges isna' gonna be so easy.'

'The accusations are all rumour and speculation,' Hart said. 'I've not heard of any real evidence beside witness reports, and you know how unreliable witnesses can be, especially after some time. Can you remember the faces of every man you've arrested, Sheriff?'

'I remember the face of every man I've killed,' Alec growled, looking Hart straight in the eyes. He held his gaze just long enough to see the first touch of uncertainty appear on the lawyer's face, before raising his glass for another drink. 'York isn't in town, I know. I guess you've got some way of keeping in touch wi' him?'

'I have,' Hart answered, lifting his chin as he recovered his poise. 'He will be in court for his trial when the date is set. However, I do not feel that it is appropriate for me to discuss my client with you any further.'

Alec nodded acknowledgement. However, he wanted to find out more about Hart if he could; to get a better feel of the man. He took another drink and let his gaze wander around the room, pausing on the framed law degree. 'Your parents must be proud of you.'

Hart's face softened. 'My mother died when I was seventeen.'

'Och! I'm sorry tae hear that.' Alec felt instant sympathy for him.

'I haven't spoken to my father in years. Nothing I did was ever good enough, compared to what he'd done. I could never measure up to his standards, what he'd achieved. But I did it!' Hart's blue

45

eyes flashed. 'I had to fight him to get the costs of my education and I had to work evenings in a store to earn money for my books and decent clothes to attend court in.' His expression changed again as he sighed. 'It was difficult, managing by myself, with no support from my family. I've achieved a lot, but you can't imagine how hard it was, struggling on my own.' He leaned back in his chair, looking sorrowful.

'I managed on my own,' Alec replied. 'I made it from enlisted man to captain in the cavalry, then sheriff of Dereham county. I had to do it on my own; the only family I had here in America were my parents, and they both died when I was fifteen.'

Hart looked surprised, then petulant. Alec had to suppress the urge to smile at the lawyer's indignation as his bout of sympathy seeking was undermined. Hart rallied, casting a pitiful look at the sheriff.

'You do understand.' He turned his hand palm up, inviting Alec to share his mood. 'It can be so lonesome when you're struggling all alone in the world.'

The deaths of his parents in the fire had been shattering, but for all his grief, Alec had never indulged in self-pity. Sympathy for Hart's own loss was warring with irritation. He abruptly decided not to play along.

'Ye should ha' joined the army,' he said briskly. 'I made some fine friends there. My deputies are ma family now.' Pointing at the photograph of the city council, Alec added. 'Your work wi' the council will help you tae settle in and feel like one of the folk here, quicker'n you can holler howdy.'

'I guess so.' Hart's tone was grudging at first, but he mustered a smile quickly. 'You're right, Sheriff. I'm doing damn well and it's all my own work. I got all this through my own efforts and I don't owe anyone anything.'

Alec nodded. He was getting rather tired of Hart's self-absorption, so he finished his whiskey in one swift swallow. 'Well, thank you for your time. I'm sure ye have things tae do, so I'll be on my way.'

He rose, and Hart stood too.

'It was good to meet you at last, Sheriff Lawson. I hope we can work together well in the future.'

'I hope so too.' Alec finished his farewells and left the lawyer's office.

Back in the outer office, the secretary looked at him and offered a shy smile. Alec raised his hat to her, and then it occurred to him that she might be able to answer a question he'd not asked Hart.

'Is Hart married?' A quick glance at her left

47

hand showed no rings, so the secretary couldn't be his wife.

'He's not married, sir. I don't think he's court-ing, but I don't know for sure. It's not my business,' she added with nice primness.

'Of course, thank you.' With a polite nod, Alec headed back out onto the street.

Strolling along the sidewalk, Alec thought over his impressions of Hart. The lawyer certainly seemed ambitious, and willing to work hard for what he wanted. His willingness to take on York's case made sense for someone determined to win a name for himself, but it still seemed like a big gamble to Alec. He admired Hart's ambition, but there seemed to be too much ambition for his taste: something about the man made him slightly uneasy. Alec shrugged; maybe it was just the way Hart had played for sympathy that grated with him. He wondered why the lawyer hadn't married. Hart seemed like the kind of man who would want a wife to provide that sympathy and admire his success – preferably a pretty one he could show off as a trophy, Alec couldn't help thinking. Then again, maybe Hart had simply been too busy working on his career to find a wife.

Alec smiled and changed direction, walking with more purpose. He knew how hard it could be to find romance, especially out on the frontier where there were so few unmarried women. In a couple of minutes, he was standing on the sidewalk outside a dry goods store, looking in through the window. The shelves along the walls held bolts of cloth of all colours, and of more kinds of cloth than Alec could identify. His attention, however, was on the young woman behind one of the long counters. Her dress was a rich blue, with a small bustle, and simple decorations of blue and gold plaid bands at the neck, wrists and hem. It was fashionable but modest, as suited the adopted daughter of the town's minister.

Alec had enjoyed watching Lily grow in confidence as she was taught literacy and domestic skills. He'd taken her out on buggy rides and to entertainments in town, enjoying showing her the world she'd missed out on during her confined life as a slave. She loved to sew, and had been delighted to get a job at the dry goods store a month back. Now, as she and her friends examined the spools of coloured thread in a glass case, she was giggling merrily. Alec had never seen her so animated; she was always demure in his presence. He watched, unnoticed, for a couple of minutes, happy at her happiness. Someday, he hoped, her domestic skills would be put to use in the house on the ranch he dreamed of buying. She would make his house into a proper home, at last: the first real home since his parents had died. Reluctantly, Alec turned away from the window and returned to the law office where he lived now.

CHAPTER FOUR

Two mornings later, as he was looking over the day's assignments for his deputies, Alec made a snap decision.

'Karl, there's a bunch of taxes tae be collected.' He handed over a list. 'Take them in any order ye like. Ethan, there's a complaint in Dronfield about a livery stable that's neglecting its horses, and one about a saloon in Narrow that's selling short measures.' Ethan received another piece of paper with Alec's neat handwriting.

'Are there any complaints about a brothel where I get to go see if the girls are giving good value?' Sam asked eagerly.

Alec gave him a pained look. 'No. There's been reports of cattle rustling out east of Potato Hill. That's less than an hour from here, so I'll come with you tae take a look.'

Karl started to say something, caught Alec's expression, and stayed quiet.

They were in the main office at the front of the building. Ethan's desk had neat piles of papers, with a jar of hair cream and a bottle of patent liver-medicine acting as paperweights. The gun rack was near his desk, and beside that was a notice board bearing a couple of circulars, some pen-cilled notes and an out-of-date poster for the local musical society. In contrast, the surface of Sam's desk was barely visible. There was an assortment of paperwork, a badly folded copy of the Lucasville Trumpeter, a deck of cards and a shockingly ugly cast-iron inkwell that had dust in its many intricate details. On the wall behind the desk, two faded, colourized pictures of showgirls were pinned loosely that rippled with interesting effect when a breeze blew in. Karl's desk was as neat as Alec's own, almost impersonal apart from a photograph of his fiancée, Renee Winter, in a silver frame. Both the frame and the silver inkstand and pen-holder were brightly polished. On the wall behind it was a larger framed photograph of the four lawmen in dress uniform, taken just before their terms of enlistment ended.

Alec straightened his shoulders. 'You three have

had tae carry ma load for me for too long. I canna do ma full share yet, but I can do a little more now, an' I will.'

Karl looked at the other two. 'If he goes, he'll be tired and cranky tonight. If he stays here, he'll fret and be cranky.'

'I say we let him go,' Ethan said. 'He may be cranky after, but he'll be tired and go to bed early. Otherwise we'll have to put up with him sulking all evening.'

Alec cleared his throat loudly. 'I'm right here, and I'm your boss, remember?'

'All right; you can come along,' Sam said.

Alec growled slightly, but otherwise ignored the comment. 'Right. Let's go and earn our money.'

Being on horseback again, and out of the city, did wonders for Alec's mood. Relaxed comfortably in Biscuit's deep saddle, he enjoyed looking about at the high prairie as they rode to Potato Hill. It was mostly farmland close to Lucasville, but as they got further from the city, the short buffalo grass was not ploughed but was ranching land, with cattle scattered across the swells and hollows of the prairie. It was refreshingly quiet too, after the bustle of the town. With the snow-capped mountains glittering in the distance, Alec felt a sense of healing out in the clean air.

'There's a few birds flying up over there,' Sam drawled, breaking the comfortable silence of nearly half an hour. 'And a mite of dust in the air.' He pointed to the northwest.

Alec could see the faint haze of dust rising from the other side of a long slope. Concentrating his attention in that direction, he caught something else too. 'I think I heard cattle,' he said. 'Maybe being moved tae a new pasture. We need to talk to the ranchers, so we might as well take a look.'

'Sure thing.'

Turning their horses, they headed to intercept the cattle.

When they crested the slope, the lawmen saw about 30 cattle being driven at a steady pace by four men. One of the riders near the head of the herd spotted them and raised a hand in greeting. The cowboys wore bandannas over their lower faces to protect themselves from the fine haze of dust raised by the cattle as they moved over the dry prairie. Alec and Sam rode down the shallower side of the slope to meet them. The cowhands had a quick, shouted discussion, the words inaudible at this distance over the hoofs and the lowing of the cattle. Two of them changed positions slightly, turning the herd more in the direction of the two lawmen.

Alec glanced briefly at the cattle but paid more attention to the cow horses, admiring the skills of horse and rider in their specialized job. After a few moments, his instinct told him something was out of place, but it took him a little while longer to realize what it was.

'They've got their bedrolls with them,' Alec said to Sam. 'They doan' need bedrolls just for changing pasture.'

'Moving them from one ranch to another?' Sam suggested. 'Those are well-grown steers; maybe they're taking them to the railroad to ship east?'

'Could be,' Alec admitted, relaxing a little.

The nearest cowhand urged his grey horse a little faster, waving one arm to indicate he wanted to talk. 'Hey, Sheriff!' he called. 'We done chased off some no-goods that was after our beef. John saw them pretty well.' He indicated the cowhand on the other side of the herd.

Alec and Sam turned their horses towards John, leaving plenty of room as they crossed the path of the herd so they wouldn't affect its movement. John waved cheerily at their approach. With their attention diverted, both lawmen were surprised by the gunshots. The steers bellowed and stampeded, urged on by the yells of the cowhands, and a couple more shots from those who had swiftly drawn their guns while the lawmen were looking towards John. Dust swelled around the herd as it charged towards the two lawmen caught in its path.

In spite of their surprise, both men reacted instantly. At a touch, both horses leapt straight into a gallop, racing to get clear of the stampeding herd. Alec felt the power of his horse as Biscuit stretched into a pounding gallop, brown mane flying in the dusty wind. The burly rustler who had spoken was racing his grey alongside the leaders, crowding them and forcing the mass of steers to turn in the same direction that the lawmen were heading. John had drawn his pistol and was shooting as they closed towards him.

Both Alec and Sam had their guns out too, now. Alec fired two quick shots just to the far side of the oncoming herd. The head of the furthermost steer jerked as a bullet ricocheted off a horn. Bellowing, it lurched away from the impact, shoving the others back in the direction of the burly rustler trying to turn them. Sam was returning fire at John. The stench of sweating, frightened cattle and the sharper smell of gunpowder hung in the dry, dusty air. Alec yelled hoarsely, firing another shot over the steers to encourage their turn. They veered away, passing just a few feet from Biscuit's haunches as the buckskin raced over the ground.

'Wheel right!' Alec ordered.

He and Sam slowed and turned their horses in near-perfect unison. The mob of steers now separated them from the first rustler, and they could see John ahead of them, and the two who had been chasing the herd from behind. These two now changed direction, moving to meet up with John.

'Halt!'

The buckskin and the paint mare both slid to a sharp halt, almost sitting on their haunches. The rustlers let off a couple more shots but the range was too long for accurate shooting with revolvers. The herd had almost passed the lawmen now. Alec wheeled his mount to see the big rustler on the grey, turning to join the others.

'They're yours,' was all he said to Sam.

Alec waited a few moments to let the herd pass completely, vaguely aware that he was slightly out of breath. When the way was clear, he urged Biscuit on again. He circled around the point where the rustlers were gathering, staying out of revolver range. Sam had stayed still, just turning his horse so it faced directly towards the rustlers and presented a narrow target. Ignoring the shots the rustlers were firing at him, he raised his Colt and sighted carefully. His first shot missed but the second rocked John back in his saddle. A couple more shots came back his way but Sam never flinched. He fired simultaneously with the second shot and hit another rustler.

Alec was riding fast again now, spiralling in towards the rustlers. He let off a quick shot, intent on drawing some of the attention away from Sam. The man on the grey yelled something to his companions and hauled his horse around in a sharp turn. The red-haired one responded, kicking his horse into a gallop and heading to join the grey. Alec bared his teeth in a humourless smile as the two rustlers began shooting at him. He was taking a risk, but was drawing on his years of experience as a soldier. Unless the rustlers were exceptional shots, it was unlikely they'd hit a fast-moving target at this range, and few outlaws liked to spend the money for bullets necessary to become a good shot.

'Charge!'

At Alec's command, Sam fired one more shot, hitting John for the second time, then his paint mare leapt forward into a gallop. John gave a cry, barely audible over the pounding of hoofs, and slid from the saddle of his restless horse. Alec and Sam both opened fire, yelling like a full-scale cavalry charge.

The redhead's nerve broke; he hauled his horse round and spurred it hard. The one on the grey followed suit, racing away after his companion. The third one dropped his gun and raised his arm in surrender, his left arm hanging limply at his side. Sam slowed up, approaching with his gun in hand. Alec pursued the fleeing pair in the hope of getting close enough for another good shot. He took a slightly different line to the rustlers, aiming to catch up with them when they changed course to avoid a slope.

Alec felt more alive than he had in months. He was in perfect union with his horse, tackling a dangerous task and challenging his nerve and skills. The part of him his mother had called his 'highland warrior' side was revelling in the action. As his spirits soared, a prairie chicken suddenly flew up from the grass, almost under Biscuit's nose. Horse and rider were equally startled. Biscuit took a leap sideways, stumbling briefly on landing. Alec stayed with his horse through the violent movement, but his weight shifted and he resorted to grabbing the pommel of the saddle. As Biscuit regained his balance, Alec found himself struggling to stay firm in the saddle. Anger at his weakness wiped out the satisfaction of a few moments before.

Tightening the reins, he pulled Biscuit to a halt. As the horse stood snorting, Alec vented his frustration by firing a last round after the escaping outlaws. Breathing heavily, and now weary, Alec thrust his gun back into its holster and turned to join Sam.

The man Sam had shot twice, John Malone, according to his injured friend, was in a bad way. Both lawmen had seen enough injuries to know that he wasn't likely to survive more than another half hour at most. Rather than transport a dying man over the saddle of a horse, they made him as comfortable as they could, in the shelter of a large hollow where they would be out of the wind. While Sam improvized a sling for the other rustler, Phil Taylor, Alec watered the horses, loosened girths and tethered them loosely to let them graze. That done, Alec sat down, disheartened by his need to rest while Sam bustled about, whistling cheerfully, as he built a small fire and raided the outlaws' supplies to brew coffee.

The strong, black brew refreshed Alec, and he relaxed gradually. Malone had sunk into deep unconsciousness, his breathing gradually fading. Taylor sat silently, his narrow face drawn with pain. He kept casting glances at his dying comrade and then looking away hurriedly. Sam had found a detective dime novel in Taylor's saddle-bags and was reading it eagerly, though his attention was never far away from his surroundings. Alec was enjoying the quiet, and simply being on the range after spending so much time in the town. Idly watching the horses, he noticed Biscuit raising his head, his ears turning towards the top of the hollow. Sam's paint, Lady, followed the movement a few moments later.

Relaxed and still somewhat weary, Alec didn't react immediately. Only when the rustlers' two horses also noticed something did he suddenly feel alarm. As Alec started to rise, two heads appeared at the rim of the hollow. The returning rustlers abandoned caution and came further into view, guns in hand.

'Sam!' Alec yelled a warning as he grabbed his own gun.

Sam dropped the book, rolling sideways. The rustlers were firing even as Alec twisted himself aside and raised his Colt. He felt a sharp sting on his upper arm as he fired with the other hand. There was nothing but a click as the hammer fell on an empty cartridge. Alec's heart leapt and time seemed to slow. The weariness and anger had distracted him: he'd forgotten to reload after the first fight. The burly rustler who'd shot at him now knew he wasn't armed and was aiming at the more dangerous target. Sam was on his knees, firing shots as fast as he could. If he were killed, Alec knew it would be his fault for failing his friend.

Fighting back a surge of panic, Alec yelled, as if commanding a cavalry charge, and hurled his useless pistol at the nearest rustler. The big outlaw saw an object flying towards his head and instinctively dodged. The gun missed, falling short of its target, but it bought Sam a few more seconds. His first two bullets had struck home, the second ripping through the red-haired rustler's head and spraying blood and bone onto the grass. Alec's diversion gave Sam enough time to change aim and fire just before the big rustler could get off a shot.

Sam hit, the impact jolting the rustler enough that his bullet went wide. The burly man dropped his gun and slumped to the ground, making pained, gurgling sounds. Blood spilled down the slope from underneath him and his body heaved as he struggled to breathe. The injured prisoner leaned over and vomited, his face pale. Alec barely spared him a glance, turning anxiously to Sam.

'Are ye all right?'

'Sure.' Sam got to his feet, inspecting himself. 'Damn, he put a hole in my jacket. What about you?' he asked, pointing at Alec's arm.

Alec glanced down, suddenly aware that his bicep was stinging. His own jacket was torn just below the shoulder, with a little blood around the edges of the tear. 'It's nobbut a scratch.' He lifted his arm and flexed his fingers to demonstrate that all was working properly.

'Good.' Sam ejected spent cartridges and replaced them as he spoke. 'We'd better get to cleaning up this mess.'

'I'm sorry,' Alec said. 'I got careless; I forgot to reload.' He shook his head. 'I put you in danger. I failed you.'

Sam smiled. 'If you hadn't come along, it would have been just little old me against the four of them. I'm a damn fine shot, but I don't reckon as I'm that good. And it was you who spotted those two coming back to bushwhack us. Buy me a drink when we get back to town and I won't tell the others you acted like a rookie in his first taste of action.'

Alec grimaced, but couldn't help smiling a little. 'Thanks.'

He took a deep breath and looked around. The burly outlaw now lay still and quiet, as did John, the first man Sam had shot, and the red-haired man. The only surviving rustler was moaning, his face wet with tears. Alec, too, had seen friends meet messy, bloody deaths, but he couldn't feel much sympathy for Taylor. If he and Sam had been the ones to die, the outlaw wouldn't have spared a moment's thought for them. Alec took no pleasure in killing, but took comfort in his belief that he was doing it for the greater good, to protect others. Right now, he had to think about pushing his weary body to help Sam with getting things sorted out here so they could return to town. Stubbornly, Alec got started.

CHAPTER FIVE

The next day, Alec spent the morning in his office, catching up with the never-ending paperwork. By lunchtime, he felt the need to get out and went to a nearby restaurant for lunch. Afterwards, he stopped by the office of Tom Clark, the town's marshal, and spent a pleasant hour gossiping about local matters. Clark couldn't offer much information about Hart, beside a complaint from a storekeeper about an unpaid bill. Hart had said the bill had been mislaid, and paid in full the same day, with fulsome apologies. Alec walked back to the law office pleased with his little excursion, but found himself in need of a rest when he got in. He reassured Mrs Andersen that he only wanted to lie down and rest his legs, and went up to lie on his bed for a few minutes.

Sometime over an hour later, Alec was downstairs again, refreshed after his unplanned nap. The kitchen welcomed him with the rich smell of hot coffee.

'Thank ye; that was good timing,' he said to Mrs Andersen, helping himself to a mug.

'Deputy Karl: he returned a few minutes ago, so I made the coffee for him.' Mrs Andersen nodded towards the front office.

Alec nodded his thanks and headed through to find his friend. He settled himself into the chair in front of Karl's desk.

'Feeling better?' Karl asked, setting down the letter he'd been reading.

Alec nodded. 'I guess Mrs Andersen told you I was resting.'

'She didn't have to; I swear you snore louder when you're resting than when you're actually sleeping.'

Alec raised an eyebrow. 'I'll pretend I dinna hear that.'

'I wish I could say the same.'

Alec snorted and sipped his coffee. 'I went out earlier,' he explained. 'Had a wee talk with Tom Clark about what's been happening locally. Asked what he knew about Hart.'

'What do you make of Hart, now you've had

time to think on him?' Karl asked.

Alec collected his thoughts. 'Like you said, he's ambitious and downright proud of it. He sure looks the part of the big-time lawyer. I reckon if anyone can get York off, Hart'll do it.'

'You think he can afford to lose a thousand dollars if York jumps bail?'

'That much has got tae be a hit for him, but I guess he's pretty sure he won't go broke if that happens. Did ye know he's on the town council?'

Karl offered a look of apology. 'I did. I remember reading about it in the paper, but I'd forgotten. Hart's definitely in the business of making himself into a player in town, isn't he?'

Alec nodded. 'I just wish I trusted him a little more. I don't see that he's done anything wrong, but he's as slick as a peeled onion.'

'Your instincts are usually right,' Karl said. 'I guess we'll have to wait and see.' He started to say something else, then paused and looked at the clock on the wall near Sam's desk. 'Sorry, Alec, I've got to go.' He swallowed the last of his coffee hastily and stood up. 'I've got an appointment at the real estate office.'

It took Alec a moment to understand the implication. 'You've found a house?'

Karl nodded, his face warming into a real smile.

'Yes, I found somewhere that Renee and I both liked and I didn't want to delay things any longer. She's been patient long enough; I thought I should make good on my promise and marry her at last.'

'Congratulations.' Alec was genuinely pleased for his friend. Karl had been engaged to Renee Winter for almost eighteen months. 'I hope everything goes well with the deal. Have ye set a date for the wedding now?'

'Not a fixed date, yet.' Karl was pulling on his coat. 'But we're thinking of September. That should give time to fix up the house and still have good weather for a honeymoon.'

'I'll see ye later, then.' Alec sipped at the coffee as he sat, feeling faintly guilty. His absence on the hunt for Alcott, and his subsequent illness, had kept Karl too busy to get on with finding a home and arranging his marriage. He envied Karl's committed relationship but had not felt himself in a hurry to marry. Now, aware that he still felt low, even after his nap, Alec felt less certain of himself. He'd long felt that marriage wasn't compatible with his risky life: he didn't want anyone he loved to experience what he'd felt after the death of his own parents.

The lingering fatigue after his injury, and subsequent illness, depressed him. Alec had been frightened by the way his weakness had led to a near-fatal error when facing the rustlers. If he retired to a horse ranch, his actions wouldn't put anyone else in danger. The thought settled in the back of his mind.

'There's a production of Macbeth on at the new Opera House next month,' Alec said, holding his page of *The Lucasville Trumpet* for Ethan to see. It was late morning, a few days after Alec's visit to see Hart. The town's newspaper had just been delivered and the two lawmen were in the main office, sharing the pages between them.

'Oh, I want to go see Miss Cerelle and her amazing transformation dances,' Ethan replied after quickly scanning the listed programme. 'I wonder if the Opera House is going to put on a production of Mazeppa? That's one of my favourites.'

'It's certainly exciting,' Alec agreed. 'I'm sure that having a near-on naked woman strapped to the side of a galloping horse is the least of the reasons ye like it.'

'I was admiring how they made it look so real, with the horse galloping on the stage and the scenery moving behind it!' Ethan protested.

Alec's reply was interrupted by the delivery of a telegram. He read it quickly and swore.

'It's not about Sam or Karl, is it?' Ethan asked anxiously.

'No. There's been an attack on a stagecoach outside of Jamestown.' Alec shook his head. 'Everyone aboard, the driver and three passengers, all dead. All murdered.'

'Could it have been Indians off their reservation?' Ethan asked. 'A bunch of young bucks gone on the warpath?'

Alec shook his head. 'It doesn't say anything much here.' He passed the telegram to Ethan. 'I've not heard anything about Indians going off reservation. We'll only find out more by going tae take a wee look. Tell Beyer to get the horses ready; I'll ride Biscuit.'

'Jamestown's a fair ride, Alec. You've not ridden that far since you outran Alcott,' Ethan reminded him, concern on his long face.

Alec hesitated. 'You're right.' Determination flashed in his dark eyes. 'We'll take the train to Dronfield, hire horses there and ride out to the stage. It'll be quicker, anyhow.'

Ethan nodded and rose. 'I'll tell Mrs Andersen what we're doing so she can tell the others.'

'Thanks.' Picking up the telegram, Alec headed for his office, his movements brisk.

*

The stagecoach had been moved to the side of the trail when Alec and Ethan arrived. A dead horse was lying nearby, a large, messy wound visible on its neck, and two other stagecoach horses were picketed on the grass at a short distance. A buckboard stood before the stage, with two men sitting underneath in the shade. One stood up as they approached, a lean man with a star-shaped badge pinned to his check shirt. He was the marshal of Pinewood Springs, Jean Lemoyne.

'I know this ain't my jurisdiction, Sheriff,' Lemoyne said to Alec. 'But I reckoned someone should get out here and take care of those poor souls and not leave them for scavengers.' He gestured to the buckboard, where a tarpaulin covered the corpses of the four victims. 'This is Fritz.' Lemoyne indicated his companion, who had a magnificent ginger moustache. 'He's the Pinewood Springs agent for the stagecoach company.'

Alec swung down from his hired horse. The cross-country ride from Pinewood Springs to this trail was the longest ride he'd done since going to arrest York, and he was aching, but he pushed his feelings aside.

'Have ye got a name for any of them yet?' he asked, heading for the buckboard.

'The driver was Phil Hartington, a decent enough feller by all accounts. Ran his stage as regular as clockwork.' Lemoyne sighed. 'They was all four lashed to the wheels of the stage and then shot, from close up, I reckon.'

Climbing into the bed of the buckboard, Alec pulled back the tarpaulin, standing back a little to let the bad smell disperse into the breeze. When he looked closer, it was easy enough to identify Hartington, the driver, by his leathery skin and his gloves. The next man, a few years younger than Alec, was probably a miner, from the dirt engrained into skin in spite of the signs that he'd washed before setting out on his trip. There was a paunchy black man with a little grey sprinkled in his close-cropped curls who looked vaguely familiar, and a bearded white man in a suit who had soiled himself, though Alec didn't know whether it was at death, or in terror during the moments before. All four had been shot in the head, though the black man had turned away at the last moment, as his wound was in the temple. Alec swatted absently at the flies that buzzed around the bloodied wounds, before methodically searching through the pockets of the dead men.

'I've never seen a stagecoach attack so brutal,' commented Ethan as he joined Alec. 'Was the stage carrying anything special?' he asked Lemoyne, who was standing nearby fanning himself with his hat.

'I asked at the bank in Pinewood Springs. They allowed as there was cash for the Diamond Girl mine on the stage. It ain't there now.'

Alec held up a pocket watch the bearded man had been wearing. 'They haven't robbed the passengers, so they weren't desperate for every last dollar. Smart enough not to take anything that might be easily identified, anyhow.' He looked over at the body of the black man. 'You recognize him, Ethan?'

Ethan's long face looked mournful, but for once it was a genuine expression. 'Yeah, bartender in that fancy saloon with the big mirror behind the bar.' He gestured in the direction of Jamestown.

'Oh, the Crossed Spurs.' Alec frowned as he thought. 'Name of Wallis; he was a sergeant in the 9th Cavalry.' He put the pocket watch back in the bearded man's pocket and looked over the corpses again. 'How much was going to the Diamond Girl?' he asked Lemoyne.

'A couple of thousand.'

'But no guard?' queried Ethan.

Lemoyne shook his head. 'They don't always when it's less than mebbe five thousand bucks.

Figures it draws less attention to there being something worthwhile on board.'

'I've seen all I want here,' Alec said.

Ethan helped him draw the tarp back over the bodies before they jumped back down from the buckboard. Alec looked around at the stagecoach and the grazing horses before turning to Lemoyne.

'That's a six-horse hitch; where are the other three?'

'Those ones were still in their harness when we got here,' the marshal said. 'The other three had been unhitched so I guess the owlhoots done took them.'

'I can't imagine they needed all three for packhorses,' Alec mused.

'Spare mounts?' Ethan suggested.

'I can't see outlaws taking the time to find which team horses were broke to ride,' Alec pointed out. 'They must have taken them as easily portable goods to sell, but why those three, and not all five?'

'I reckon the ones they stole didn't have the company brand,' said Fritz, heaving himself to his broad feet. 'Not all of our horses do, but the pair they left do.'

Alec looked over at the horses, noting the Circle SL brand on the hip, and nodded. Moving to

74

examine the dead horse, he saw the large wound was from a shotgun, but there were a couple of other bullet wounds on its neck and shoulder. It was a grey horse, so the large patches of dried blood stood out shockingly on its near-white coat. The blast had hit low on the neck and from the amount of blood on the horse and the dirt of the trail, a major blood vessel had been hit. Alec felt a sad relief in knowing that it must have died quickly. Pushing aside his anger at the pointless death, he considered the position of the wounds and the size of the horse.

'The grey, was it the nearside lead?' he asked Fritz. The first pair of the six horses in a hitch was usually lighter in build than the other four.

When Fritz nodded, Alec turned to study the trail and surroundings. Ethan came to join him.

'They shot a lead horse to bring the stage to a halt,' Alec said, frowning slightly as he shared his thoughts. 'The stage was heading towards Jamestown and they shot the nearside horse, so they must ha' been on that side of the trail, an' they had tae be pretty close for a shotgun to leave that kind o' wound. I'm guessing they were around there.' He pointed to an outcropping of rocks among the trees, some twenty feet from the side of the trail.

Alec and Ethan walked alongside the trail, studying the marks on its surface as they went. The ground was hard and marked by the passage of many wheels and hoofs, but they picked out splashes of blood from the injured horse where it had staggered along before collapsing. Reaching the rocks, Alec and Ethan searched the area carefully, finding traces of the men who had waited there.

'Used match and a couple of cigarette stubs,' Ethan reported, showing his finds to Alec.

Alec sniffed at the cigarette stubs 'Durham, but that's common enough. They left their horses tied in those birches.' He pointed to the spot he'd investigated. 'Shadier and more out of sight than behind this outcrop.'

'Could you tell how many?'

Alec shook his head. 'I'd guess about four, but there's no way for me to be sure.'

Ethan looked back towards the stagecoach. 'I never heard of a stage robbery where everyone aboard was killed like that, and I can't think of any off-hand where it was so deliberate.'

'They didn't want to leave witnesses,' Alec said grimly. 'And don't care about getting the law riled at them.'

'Don't care none for the folks they killed either.

76

Most outlaws just aren't that callous.'

'I think it was York,' Alec said flatly.

Ethan looked at him, and then nodded. 'Makes sense.'

Alec started walking back along the trail. 'Let's see if we can find anything around the stage. Then I'll send Lemoyne and Fritz back to Pinewood Springs. We'd better go on to Jamestown tae talk to folk there.' Alec stubbornly ignored his desire to lie down for a while.

'With you, boss.' Ethan's expression told Alec he wasn't fooling his friend.

It was Ethan who found the cluster of ejected cartridges. He brought them to Alec, holding them in the palm of his hand. 'I found them together; I guess someone reloaded after killing the witnesses. They look some smaller than standard.'

Alec picked one up and then slipped a bullet from the loops on his gunbelt to compare. 'You're right.' A tight, dangerous smile came onto his face. 'These are .41 calibre long Colt cartridges, for the Thunderer. York carries a Thunderer, remember? We'll get that noose tighter round his neck with these!' He tossed the cartridge into the air and caught it, laughing with satisfaction.

CHAPTER SIX

'Are you all right?' Karl asked as Alec made his way across the kitchen the next morning.

'I'm no' an invalid,' Alec responded indignantly. He'd been hoping that it wasn't too obvious how stiff he was after the previous day's riding.

Karl raised an eyebrow. 'You were exhausted when you got back yesterday.'

'You fell asleep on the train back from Pinewood Springs,' Ethan added, sitting down with a plate of ham and beans.

'Your conversation never was up to much,' Alec retorted, heading for the coffee pot.

Sam laughed. 'If'n I'm ever having trouble sleeping, I just imagine Ethan's telling me about his bad stomach or the latest cure-all he's trying, and I'm soon out like a light.'

'An' you make just as much sense asleep as awake,' Ethan retorted.

'Quit bickering, children,' Alec interjected, pouring himself a mug of strong coffee. He turned to Karl, and pretended not to notice as a dishcloth flew from Sam towards Ethan, just in the corner of his vision. 'I'm going tae call on Hart later this morning and ask him to get York tae come in so's I can talk to him.'

'You think he'll cooperate?' Karl asked.

Alec took a sip of his coffee. 'Hart will say the right things; it's in his interest. I'm no' so sure York will.' He made a sour face. 'I really doan' like that bastard.'

'Which one? The outlaw or the lawyer?'

Alec laughed. 'Where there's one, there's the other.'

'We'd be out of work without them!' Sam protested.

'I'd be happy if there was no need for anyone to do this job,' Alec said, moving towards the stove. 'Meanwhiles, there's plenty for you fun-loving idlers tae do, so let's eat and get on wi' it.'

'Spoilsport,' Sam grumbled, passing him the frying pan.

First business of the day for Alec was the usual routine of a short discussion with his deputies before setting them their first tasks of the day. When they were about their work, he collected letters, applications and notices that had arrived and took them into his own office to read and sort them. Alec looked at the pile of paperwork resentfully. He'd always had to deal with it, but somehow it seemed more aggravating than before. It seemed that paperwork was all he was fit for now. Taking a deep breath, Alec dutifully applied himself to it.

When everything had been looked at, immediate issues dealt with and the rest filed for later attention, Alec settled down to writing up more detailed information on the stagecoach ambush. He'd been too tired to make more than the briefest notes after returning from Pinewood Springs. When he'd finished, Alec got out his previous files about York and Hart and re-read them. He spread the papers on his desk, glancing from one to another as he formulated his thoughts on how to approach the lawyer. After a few minutes, Alec abruptly gathered the pages together, put them back in their file and stood up, reaching automatically for jacket, hat and gunbelt.

Hart was busy with a client when Alec arrived at his office, but the sheriff elected to sit and wait. He watched the secretary using the typewriter, fascinated by the clacking of the keys, the whirring of the mechanisms sliding, and looking forward to the ding of the bell at the end of each line. After a few minutes, he realized his attention seemed to be making the young secretary nervous for some reason; every so often she would peep a glance at him, which often seemed to be followed by a clash of keys in the typing. Alec politely directed his attention to the street outside the window.

Soon afterwards, Hart's client left. He was a local rancher that Alec knew had been having disputes with a neighbour over barbed wire fences. As a legal case, it seemed rather minor for an ambitious lawyer who had taken on a challenging criminal case, but Alec supposed that Hart regarded it as bread and butter money. When he went through to the lawyer's office, Hart smiled and offered him a glass of whiskey.

'No, thank ye. I'm here on business this time.' Alec sat down.

Hart steepled his fingers together. 'How may I be of assistance, Sheriff?'

'I want tae speak to Saul York. I want ye to contact him and ask him tae come an' see me as soon as possible.'

'Might I enquire why?'

Alec gave him a considering look before speaking. 'Have ye heard about the attack on the

81

Jamestown stage yesterday?'

Hart nodded. 'A brutal crime, it sounded like.' He frowned across the desk. 'Are you accusing my client of being involved?'

'I'm not accusing anyone.' Alec was careful to keep his tone neutral.

'But you want to speak to York in connection with the stage attack?' Hart persisted.

'I do. He's out on bail, thanks to you. You're the one who knows how to contact him, so I want you to do just that, so he can answer my enquiries.'

'The attack on the Jamestown stage is nothing to do with any of the charges my client is accused of, so I am not acting on his behalf in respect of that crime. Therefore I see no requirement for me to contact him in regard to it. If you suspect him of involvement in it, you will have to track him down yourself.'

Alec's eyes narrowed. 'Obstructing the course of justice is a crime in itself. If you know how tae get hold of York, and refuse to aid me, the judge may not take to kindly tae that.'

'That sounds like a threat, Sheriff Lawson,' Hart said, his voice cool, though his eyes betrayed anger.

'It's a wee reminder,' Alec replied, not flinching from Hart's gaze.

'Why, specifically, do you want to talk to York in connection with the Jamestown stage?'

'I can't tell ye. But ma investigation's in its very early stages. If York volunteers some useful information, that may be taken into consideration later in his trial,' Alec added as a concession.

Hart leaned back in his chair. 'A major robbery takes place and you immediately assume that my client is somehow connected with it. There are other gangs of outlaws operating in Colorado, Sheriff.'

' "Other outlaws". . . . Ye admit then that York is an outlaw?' Alec pounced immediately.

Hart's lips narrowed as he realized his mistake. 'You are assuming that my client is associated with this robbery without giving grounds for your suspicion,' he continued firmly. 'Demanding that he defends himself to you after every crime that takes place is unnecessary, and potentially harassment. I'm sorry, but you can't act that way, Sheriff.'

Alec felt the sudden impulse to draw his gun and shoot the superior look from Hart's face, but his hand remained still. 'If ye hadn't gotten York out on bail, I'd ken where he was, and ha' no need tae be questioning him about this attack,' he growled, his accent getting thicker. 'An' it was no' a mere *robbery*; it was a *murder*! Four men tied up and shot in the face wi' no mercy. Four lives taken, four men dyin' in terror for money that weren't e'en theirs!'

'My client wasn't involved,' Hart protested, though more weakly than before, his self-assurance rattled by Alec's display of temper.

'I still need ye tae tell him tae come an' talk tae me.'

Hart found himself on the receiving end of the full force of Alec's glare, the controlled anger of a cavalry captain faced with a disobedient underling. He yielded.

'I'll get word to York,' Hart promised. 'I can't say how long he'll be, but I'll impress on him the importance of not delaying.'

'Good.' Alec rose with a sharp movement. 'Thank ye for your time,' he added, with precise courtesy.

Hart nodded. 'We're both aiming to serve the law,' he said.

Alec thought that one of them had better aim than the other, but he kept his thoughts from his face. He marched out, nodding politely to the secretary as he passed. He moved away from the front of the lawyer's office and then halted and sighed deeply, trying to ease the tension built up in his body. He appreciated that Hart was looking out for his client's interests, but the officious obstruction of his investigation into a set of four callous murders left him simmering with anger. Having to rely on Hart to contact York made him feel helpless, something he'd never liked.

Alec shook his head, as if to clear away the negative thoughts that circled him. He needed a distraction. His first thought was to saddle Biscuit and go for a ride, but although his stiffness had eased, he knew he needed to take things easy today. His weakness was another annoyance, brooding at the back of his mind. Two women brushed past him as he stood on the sidewalk, chattering about a new hat one had seen in a store window. Alec smiled suddenly, and began walking with new purpose.

The dry goods store was fairly busy when Alec entered but he quickly found Lily at a till, serving a neatly dressed woman who was buying buttons. Alec moved into line behind the woman, waiting for Lily to be free.

With the transaction finished, the woman turned abruptly and came face to face with him. Startled recognition flashed in her brown eyes. 'Alec!'

'Eileen.'

She was tall for a woman, nearly the same height

he was. Slender and graceful, Eileen Wessex was beautiful. A childless, young widow, she had moved to Lucasville the summer before, to teach school. Now, her intelligent eyes scanned Alec's face with concern.

'I heard you've been very sick,' she said.

Alec shrugged. 'Aye, I had pneumonia. I've no' seen you in a long time,' he added warmly. 'Are ye keeping well?'

'Yes, thank you.' Eileen glanced back to Lily, who was by the till, watching them both. Lily smiled and greeted Alec in a tone of pleasant surprise.

'I must be going,' Eileen said, pushing the packet of buttons into her bag. 'There's plenty to do at home during the summer recess.' She started to move, then paused. 'I'm glad you're well again,' she said impulsively, and then walked away quickly without looking back.

Alec watched her as she left the shop, a little puzzled by her abrupt departure.

'Alec?'

He turned, smiling back at Lily, feeling a warm rush of affection for the young woman.

'I did not know you knew Mrs Wessex,' Lily said, tilting her head in enquiry.

'Aye. Not long after she moved to town last year, this miner, Dench, started in to pestering her. He was following her an' waiting outside the school-house when she left, nearly every day. I had tae arrest him in the end. O' course, I got to know Eileen while Dench was bothering her.'

In fact, Alec had become friends with her, escorting Eileen to some concerts and taking her out for a buggy ride into the mountains. It occurred to him briefly that he never seemed to run into her any more, but then Lily asked him why he'd come into the store, and his attention was diverted in a most pleasurable little chat.

Saul York strolled in through the door of the sheriff's office three days later. He meandered over to Sam's desk, drew on his cigarette, and exhaled a cloud of smoke in the deputy's face.

'I heard y'all wanted to see me?' he drawled.

'Yeah,' Sam replied. 'Preferably at the end of a rope.'

York grinned. 'Well, we can't always get what we want, can we? Now, why don't you go tell the sheriff I'm here?'

Sam gave him a cold look and went to notify Alec.

When the two lawmen came back from the sheriff's office, York had seated himself, leaning back with his feet up on Karl's desk. The stub of his cigarette had been stubbed out on the leather blotter pad.

'Get your feet off there,' Alec barked.

'I'm comfortable like this,' York stated. 'I come all this way because you asked; I got a right to make myself comfortable.'

'And I've got the right tae insist ye take your feet off the furniture in ma place of work,' Alec told him sharply.

York did as he was told, sulkiness in every movement.

Alec moved closer, looking down on York in the chair. 'Where have ye been staying?'

York cocked his head to one side. 'My law-dog told me I don't need to answer that.'

Alec considered this. 'Yes, your lawyer. Your expensive lawyer. He's not defending you out of the goodness of his heart. He going to expect repayment. How are you going to pay Hart?'

'I got money.' York took out another cigarette and lit it, holding it in his left hand.

'How did you get it?'

'I won it gambling. I won a few hundred bucks on roulette an' I'll get some more before it comes to trial time.'

Alec folded his arms. 'Roulette, eh? Where? Which saloon?'

'The Silver Wheel in Estes Park.'

Estes Park was up at the northern border of Alec's jurisdiction. The Silver Wheel was a biggish place, with rooms to rent and a lively stage show, but it wasn't fancy. Alec wasn't convinced that it was the sort of place where bets would often run into the hundreds, but then funny things happened sometimes when gambling. He decided not to press further about York's money at the moment.

'Show me your gun.'

York raised an eyebrow, then smiled. 'You want to see my revolver?' His right hand dropped casually to his holster.

'Aye, and doan' get any funny ideas,' Alec said. 'Ye don't have tae give it to me, just show it. Don't point it at me, an' keep your finger well away from the trigger. Sam get pretty jumpy when folks aim guns at his friends, and he can get you as dead as beef before you even know he's drawing.' Alec half-smiled, radiating complete confidence.

York turned to look at Sam, who had quietly donned his gunbelt, and stood a few paces away, watching with the focused readiness of a hunter that's spotted its prey. Sam smiled cheerfully at the outlaw, without looking any less deadly. York scowled briefly, looking like a petulant child

89

denied a second cookie. Alec successfully repressed the urge to grin. With exaggerated care, York drew his gun, keeping his fingers well away from the trigger, and held it towards Alec. It was a Colt Thunderer .41, a double action revolver. Unlike most other revolvers, it could be fired without needing to cock the hammer first, which was why Alec had been so specific about York keeping his finger away from the trigger.

'Thank ye,' Alec nodded.

Scowling, York re-holstered his revolver. 'You made me come here just so's you could see my gun?' He glanced back and forth between the two lawmen, puzzled and suspicious.

'Well, I like tae know you aren't too far away; you got a trial to attend, after all.'

York sat upright. 'Is that all? I got better places to be.'

'Since you've come all this way, you might as well answer a few questions,' Alec said. 'I'm guessing you've heard about the robbery of the Jamestown stage?'

York slumped back into his chair. 'I heard some about it, yeah.'

'Everyone on the stage was killed,' Alec said. 'The robbers only got a two thousand dollar payroll, but they killed everyone to get it.'

York took a long draw on his cigarette, exhaling the smoke at leisure. 'They was strangers to me. I don't care too hard 'bout them.'

'They had names,' Sam said coldly, moving closer. 'The driver was Phil Harrington.'

'Wallis was a bartender,' Alec said. 'Maybe he served you one time.'

'There was a miner, Joe Crewe.'

'And Hickson was a teacher,' Alec continued. 'He came out west in the spring for the sake of his health. He was on his way to the mineral springs in Jamestown.'

'Too late for the springs to do him any good,' York remarked.

Alec refused to let York's callous response get to him. 'He was married.'

'So was the guard,' Sam added.

'There was no guar. . . .' York stopped abruptly, then, with a quick glance at Alec, continued. 'The newspaper reports never mentioned no guard.' He smirked, pleased with himself for avoiding the trap.

CHAPTER SEVEN

Alec smiled humourlessly. He hadn't been relying on catching out York that way, and as the outlaw had said, the deaths of those on the stagecoach had been covered in the newspapers.

'All the same, four people were killed,' he said. 'Which was a mistake by the outlaws.'

'You see,' Sam said, moving in so he was standing on York's other side. 'Stealing a payroll is one thing; we'd always be looking for anyone who did that.'

'Murder is another thing,' Alec explained. 'Let alone four murders at once.'

'Rewards go up a lot for finding and catching killers,' Sam said.

'And I get real angry at scum who tie innocent folk tae stagecoaches an' shoot them like rabid dogs.'

With statements being fired at him from two directions, York was turning his head back and forth as Alec and Sam spoke in turn. The pace of the conversation was increasing, giving him less time to think.

'So y'all can see why the killer made a mistake,' Sam said, looking cheerful. 'They got Alec here mad at them, much more so than if they just took the money. Why, he's mad enough to chew nails and spit rivets.'

'There'll be bounty hunters after them, too,' Alec added.

'And all for just a couple of thousand dollars.' Sam shook his head, looking at York. 'That ain't much really, is it?'

'Don't forget there were the horses,' Alec interrupted.

'That's so. They stole three of the stage horses.'

'They were smart enough to take the ones that weren't branded, anyway,' Alec said.

'Could have had four horses, 'cept they stopped the stage by shooting the wheeler.'

'Not the wheel . . .' York cut his scornful correction short. 'I heard it was a lead horse,' he blustered.

Alec grinned mirthlessly. 'That wasna' in the papers: I asked them not tae mention a horse

93

getting shot.'

York surged to his feet. 'I didn't read it: I heard it someplace. It musta been someone from the stage company who talked about it. I didn't have to come here to talk to you, an' I'm not staying.' Scowling at both lawmen, he stamped from the office, slamming the door behind himself.

Sam's merry laughter was loud enough for the outlaw to hear as he retreated.

Alec chuckled too. 'Aye, it's a shame we've no way o' recording him when he gives himself away. Mind, even if we did, it's not strong enough evidence on its own. It's as sure as sin that he was there, but he *coulda*' heard those things from others.'

Sam nodded. 'Is there enough reasonable suspicion to get an arrest warrant, you think? If he was behind bars again, then either Hart would have to put up more money for bail, or else York would be rotting away where he couldn't hurt anyone while he waited for trial.'

'I don't reckon so,' Alec said slowly. 'Not yet.'

They were still talking about York a few minutes later when Ethan came in, carrying a bottle of blood tonic from the drugstore.

'I saw Hart a short while ago,' he remarked, after greeting the others.

'Was he with York?' Alec asked.

Ethan shook his head. 'He was in the Dereham County Bank, depositing some money. Looked to be a fair stack of new bills.'

'New bills?' Alec asked, sliding off the corner of Karl's desk, where he'd been perched. 'You don't often see stacks of new bills outside of bank safes and payrolls.'

'Well, they looked new from where I was standing,' Ethan said. 'But I wasn't watching closely. There could be an honest explanation that don't mean anything bad,' he added with characteristic melancholy.

Sam grinned. 'I done told you, you need spectacles.'

'All the same, it could be worth looking into,' Alec said thoughtfully. 'I reckon as I'll go pay Hart a wee visit.'

'Want me to come along?' Sam asked eagerly. 'I could wait in front with his secretary whiles you talk to Hart and keep an eye out for York.'

Alec snorted. 'Your eyes would be on the secretary. York could walk right through the office and you'd never notice. You'd better get back to the paperwork on that tax auction next week. I need tae know how long it's likely to take.'

'Spoilsport,' Sam muttered insincerely as he

returned to his desk.

When Alec arrived at Hart's office, the secretary informed him that her boss was not in.

'I'm afraid he left about half an hour ago. He said he had to do something in town, and then he'd be away for the rest of today and tomorrow morning as well. I've got some letters to type, and I'm to answer any enquiries, if I can,' she confided.

'Thank you, Miss. . . ?'

'Miss Dodd,' she replied, with a becoming touch of colour in her cheeks as she looked at him.

Alec's first reaction had been disappointment at not being able to see Hart, but an opportunity just had occurred to him. It wasn't strictly honest, but Alec had occasionally bent the rules before in the pursuit of a greater justice. He smiled at Miss Dodd.

'When I was here before, I think I left ma cigarette case in Mr Hart's office. Do ye think I could pop in and have a wee look for it?'

Miss Dodd smiled back. 'Why, as it's you, Sheriff, I'm sure that would be all right.'

'Thank you.' With another smile, Alec slipped into the lawyer's office before she could change her mind.

Shutting the door after himself, Alec hesitated as he looked around. He didn't own a cigarette case, as he only smoked the occasional cigar, but it had been a plausible excuse to gain entry to Hart's office. After a moment, he went to the filing cabinet and tried the top drawer cautiously. It wasn't locked, and slid out quietly. The lacy curtain over the small window at the back of the room let in enough light for him to see the contents, while still providing privacy. Alec swiftly opened and closed one drawer after another.

There were fewer papers in the cabinet than Alec had expected. He lifted the files out one by one, glancing through the papers just enough to get an idea of the subject without picking up too much confidential information. What he saw seemed to be mostly civil stuff: property disputes, a case for slander and a couple of wills. Alec only saw a couple of criminal cases, one was defending a horse thief and the other was a successful defence of a man accused of robbing a grocery store. It was minor stuff in comparison to York's crimes. Alec wondered where else Hart had practised law: he might have taken bigger cases elsewhere.

Searching further, he found invoices from a local furniture shop for the office fittings. It was a hefty sum, all on credit. Further invoices for clothes, liquors and cigars showed Hart had made quite an outlay on his business in the few months since arriving in Lucasville. Most had been paid, but a couple of more recent ones were still outstanding. Aware of time passing, Alec closed up the filing cabinet quietly. He took a quick look at the framed law certificate, noting the college Hart had graduated from. A quick peek in the desk drawers yielded nothing useful, like a way of contacting York. On his last glance around, Alec spotted the two used glasses by the decanters. A quick check confirmed that both had been used for whiskey. Alec half-smiled: whoever the last guest was, he wasn't someone Hart needed to impress by drinking the more expensive brandy.

Leaving the private office, Alec stopped by Miss Dodd's desk. 'I couldna' find it,' he said. 'I guess I'll have tae look elsewhere.'

'Oh, I'm sorry. Is there anything I can do to help?' Miss Dodd looked at him hopefully.

Alec shook his head. 'I'm sure it'll be fine; there's no need tae mention it to Hart. There is one thing you could tell me though.'

'Yes?'

'Did Saul York visit here this morning?'

'Why, yes. He came to see Mr Hart maybe an hour ago.'

'So just before Hart left for the day?'

She smiled. 'That's right.'

'Thank you.' Alec returned the smile. 'I'm verra glad for your help, Miss Dodd. Mr Hart's surely done the right thing tae trust you to look after the office in his absence.'

She coloured in the prettiest way as Alec nodded to her before leaving. He walked back to his office briskly, keen to make notes on what he'd seen and consider his next move.

Two days later, Sunday, Alec was in quite a different mood when he appeared in the lawmen's living quarters after lunch. His hair was well brushed, his cream shirt was nearly new and there was a distinct spring in his step.

Sam glanced at Ethan. 'I reckon our boss's going courting.'

Ethan carefully stacked the plate he'd just finished drying. 'He's all gussied up, that's for sure.'

'Why, I swear that shirt's been ironed recent.'

Steadfastly ignoring them, Alec paused by Karl, who was relaxing in his chair with a book. 'You're having dinner with Renee and her brother this evening?'

Karl nodded. 'I'll be back about eleven.'

'I'll see you later, then.' Alec headed for the door to the front office.

'Take care,' Sam called. 'You don't want to go

getting all mussed up afore you even see Miss Lily, now. She might not recognize you if'n you show up looking like you usually do.'

Alec resisted the urge to slam the door behind himself.

Half an hour later, he was at the reins of a hired buggy, Lily on the seat beside him. Ahead, the foothills of the Rockies swelled with towering peaks of the mountains beyond. The buggy rolled swiftly on the packed dirt of the trail, behind the matched pair of quick-stepping horses.

'It's grand tae be out here, isn't it?' Alec said with satisfaction.

'Yes, I like it,' Lily answered, smiling sweetly at him.

'I thought we'd go past Lyons and closer tae the mountains,' he said.

'Oh, lovely. Mary said that if you go the South Sain' Vrain and go Coffintop Gulch, there are some lovely views.' Lily spoke carefully, articulating the words as clearly as she could. Her English had improved immensely since she'd lived with the Browns, but she still had a distinct accent, with a tendency to swallow hard sounds at the end of words.

'That's right,' Alec agreed. 'We'll do that then.' He racked his brains for a few moments. 'I doan' think I ken who Mary is,' he admitted.

'Mary Babcoc'; her father paints houses and does decorations inside them,' Lily explained as best she could. 'She joined the Young Ladies Society at the church las' month and I help her choose materials for a new dress she is making. She go' very pretty blue lawn, with narrow pink and green stripes.'

Lily continued to chatter away as they drove. Alec was delighted that she was settling in and making friends, though it occurred to him in passing that he knew very few of the people she was talking about. However, it was pleasant just to hear how happy she was. When they had passed through Lyons and into the wilder country, Lily talked less, gazing about at the scenery instead. She was asking about the peaks in the distance when Alec halted the buggy.

'A wee moment,' he said, applying the brake. Alec slipped out of the buggy and was back a few seconds later holding a pair of bright red flowers he'd spotted near the trees.

Lily accepted them with a smile. 'Lilies,' she said, caressing the stems. 'Like the firs' flower you gave me.' That had been just after Alec and his deputies had rescued her from the bootleggers who had owned her, on the first stage of her journey to a new life. 'Thank you,' she whispered, looking at him with such devoted hero-worship that Alec blushed slightly.

He shook the reins. 'Let's get to that view and have a bite tae eat.'

Soon afterwards, they were settled in a lovely glade, with the gentle murmur of a creek nearby and the sounds of the buggy horses eating. Alec lay on his back in the grass, arms folded behind his head, watching Lily as she sat on the checked rug.

'This is beautiful,' she said, gazing about with interest.

'Aye,' Alec agreed lazily, thinking what a lovely picture she made in her surroundings.

'I am so grateful to you,' she said, picking up the lilies and holding them to herself. 'I have so happy life now.'

'You deserve it.'

'I love being in Lucasville. There is so many things to see and to do. Never have I ha' such richness in my life. I see so many people in the store. I go to church an' the church socials. I have been to two parties! And concerts. I di' not know about all these things before, but the town is full of them.' She looked over at him, her delicate face radiantly happy.

'You like visiting the country, though, don't

you?' he asked.

Lily nodded. 'It is nice to look at, but I spent so much time before in small houses with men an' no one else. Now I am in the town an' I feel safe there.'

'Of course.' Alec changed the subject. 'I'm going tae Estes Park tomorrow; that's way up higher into the mountains.'

'Oh . . . is it pretty?' Lily asked.

'Aye, but that's no' why I'm going,' he replied, sitting up. 'I'm going tae check on a story that Saul York told me about how he got some money. He says he won it playin' roulette, but I'm no' so sure.'

Lily frowned as she thought. 'Is he the bad man you chase before you were sick?'

'That's right.'

She asked a couple of questions about why York had been released after his arrest, but Alec soon saw that she wasn't really attending to his explanation of bail and due process, even though he was giving a simple version. Instead, he got up.

'How about taking a wee walk in the trees before we eat?' he suggested, offering her his hand.

'I would like that, Sheriff Alec,' she answered, letting him help her up.

'Good.' Alec smiled as he led her into the shade of the birch trees.

The walk, the picnic and the drive home were pleasant, but as Alec returned the buggy and horses to the livery stable, he couldn't help feeling slightly disappointed with his day. Lily was as beautiful and enchanting as ever, but he hadn't enjoyed himself as much as he'd expected to. There seemed to be a slight unease he'd not felt before and it made him uncomfortable. Pushing his concern to the back of his mind, Alec focused on the day ahead.

CHAPTER EIGHT

'You can see why the tourists come here,' Alec remarked to Karl, as they strolled up the wide main street of Estes Park. He gestured towards a fine hotel. 'Have you and Renee thought about coming here for your honeymoon?'

Karl shook his head. 'We're thinking of going to Washington, to get some art and culture. We'd both like to see the Smithsonian Institution and the National Museum that opened a couple of years ago.'

'It does sound interesting,' Alec admitted. 'But it's a fair way tae travel.'

Karl smiled. 'You just can't imagine anyone preferring a city to a mountain, can you, you stubborn old Scot?'

'I like a wee bit of culture as much as anyone,'

Alec protested. 'I just doan' see the need tae travel two thousand miles for it. Anyway, we got work tae do now.' He gestured at the Silver Wheel saloon to their left. It was one of the largest buildings around, two full storeys high, with a silver-painted wagon wheel fixed above the main door.

It seemed dim inside after the bright morning sun on the street. The saloon looked much as Alec remembered it from his visit the previous year. Although it was just around noon, the place was fairly busy. A few people were eating, but most were drinking and gambling, out to enjoy themselves. After a quick glance around assessing the layout, Alec led the way to the gaming tables clustered along the wall opposite the bar. Passing the keno table and the blackjack, he made his way round the long roulette table to the operator. The ball was whirring round the wheel, watched intently by half a dozen gamblers, with nearly as many onlookers crowded around. Alec pushed his way in, Karl behind him, and watched as the ball clattered its way into a slot.

'Red nineteen,' the operator called.

Alec waited until the bets had been paid off then caught the operator's attention. 'I need tae talk to ye for a couple of minutes.'

The operator heaved a short sigh. He had a

narrow face, the length exaggerated by a hairline that had receded almost to the top of his head. 'Isn't there anyone else here who can help you, Sheriff?'

'I'm interested in someone who claims he won a lot of money here at roulette,' Alec said, backing his request with a firm stare.

The controller sighed again, and waved to the players. 'I'm halting for a few minutes.'

Some of the crowd drifted away to the bar or other games, others started talking. A man in a plaid shirt thumped the table.

'Play on, dammit! I got a hot run here.'

A quick nod from Alec was all it needed for Karl to go talk to the protester.

'Have ye had any big wins here in the last month or so?' Alec asked the operator.

'How big?'

'Upwards of a few hundred bucks.'

The roulette controller rubbed one hand over the bald area at the front of his head. 'Well, there are a feller won some five hundred here a couple of weeks back.'

'Only five hundred?'

The operator nodded, and grinned, displaying teeth browned from chewing tobacco. 'Won five hundred playing roulette and lost four hundred and fifty on faro.' He pointed a thumb in the direction of the faro table. 'He were madder'n a wet hen when that last ace came up on the lose pile.'

Alec frowned. 'You ever see Saul York here? A little taller than me, fair hair and bright blue eyes. Got a bunch of old smallpox scars on his face,' Alec added. 'Carries a Colt Thunderer and a bowie knife in a brown gunbelt.'

'I seen him. Once was plenty.'

'Has he won big playing roulette here?'

The operator shook his head. 'He don't play roulette much. I've seen him play faro some more, but mostly he's drinking and manhandling the girls.' He lowered his voice. 'No one here likes him much but they don't dare say nothing: he's got a mean temper, York has.'

Alec thanked the roulette operator for his time. Leaving the table, he joined Karl and took a look around the saloon.

'York lied to us about where he got the money,' he told his deputy.

'Am I supposed to be surprised?' Karl enquired mildly.

Alec snorted a laugh. 'I'd be surprised if you were. But he does come here. We need tae ask around, see if we can find anyone who can tell us something about his. . . .'

A saloon girl hurrying down the stairs had caught his attention. He stopped speaking as she made for the bar, calling for someone urgently.

'Davy! Davy! You gotta come upstairs right away!'

Alec headed towards her, Karl behind him. A bearded man, short, but almost as broad as tall, passed a full beer glass to a customer.

'I love you, Sue, but I ain't got time for doing that right now,' he replied, laughing. 'I gotta serve beer to these ugly souls instead.'

The men around him laughed too, passing bawdy comments, but made way as Sue pushed through to face Davy over the bar. She slapped a palm on the bar top in front of him.

'There's blood coming out from under the door of room 10!'

The blunt announcement drew exclamations from those around.

'Show me,' Alec ordered.

The saloon girl turned and stared blankly at him for a moment, then saw the badge on his jacket. 'Yes, Sheriff.' She glanced at Davy, who gestured for her to go.

'I'm coming up too,' the barman said, heading for the bar exit.

Sue trotted back the way she'd come, Alec and

Karl right with her. They left a buzz of talk around the bar as Davy hurried to catch up with them.

'What did ye see?' asked Alec as they climbed the stairs.

'I was coming down to start my shift,' Sue explained, a little breathlessly. 'I saw something spreading across the floor, dark liquid, and I guessed it was wine. 10 is a guest room and I figured someone had taken a girl up there with some wine. It's kinda early for that but maybe they weren't in town for long. When I got closer, I saw it was thicker than wine and then I smelled it.' She paused, and shivered slightly. 'I guess it was a lot of blood, to have spilled out like that.' Her voice was suddenly fainter.

The stairs came out onto a cross-corridor running the length of the building, with a window at each end, currently open to let a breeze through. Alec glanced both ways and saw the dark stain spreading across the uncarpeted boards in front of a closed door.

'Wait here,' he told Sue, who made no objection.

Drawing their guns, Alec and Karl approached the door, careful not to tread in the blood. Davy trailed them at a short distance. Alec paused, turning his ear to the door.

'I doan' hear anything.' He banged once on the door and waited a few moments. When there was no sound from within, he turned the knob with his free hand and pushed cautiously. The door opened a couple of feet before coming up against something. Alec peered into the gap. 'I can see one body.' After another quick look to establish the size of the blood spill, he slipped carefully through the gap, gun ready for action.

Alec moved in far enough to let Karl follow, scanning the room as he went. It was a large room, with a double bed against one wall with a small chest of drawers beside the headboard. A wooden chair stood under the window, a match to the two other chairs by a small table in the corner near the door. One chair was overturned, lying alongside the body of a skinny man with long side-whiskers. The body behind the door was of an average-sized, average-height man with short, light brown hair. Both wore undistinguished range clothes and gun-belts. There was a blood-smeared knife on the floor beside the skinny man, and another under the hand of the second man. Most of the drying blood had come from the gash in the second man's throat.

The room smelt of tobacco, blood and whiskey, the latter from an almost empty bottle on the table, along with some playing cards and coins.

'I've seen men fall out over cards before,' Karl said. 'But both men dying? Usually one at least gets away, even if they're bleeding.'

Alec knelt by the skinny one and checked for a pulse. 'Dead, but still pretty warm. All that blood's pretty fresh, too.'

Karl stuck his head out of the door to address Davy. 'See if there's anyone in the neighbouring rooms that might have heard an argument.'

Alec looked around at the room, then at the corpse he was next to, trying to work out how the fight might have taken place. 'This one looks familiar.' He paused, remembering. 'Mutt Hingis, wanted for armed robbery. He must ha' been stabbed first, then slashed your victim's throat before he collapsed. It must have been a deep slash tae bleed out as much as that; he couldna' stabbed Hingis afterwards.'

Karl inspected the wound in his victim's neck cautiously. 'Yeah, this is a pretty big gash.'

Alec looked around again: he had a gnawing sensation that something wasn't quite right with the picture they were forming. Karl saw his expression and kept quiet, letting him think. As well as the pool of blood that had seeped under the door, there were splashes on the floor and wall, indicating where the unnamed man had been standing when his throat was cut. Alec bent over Hingis to look more closely.

'He canna be the killer,' Alec said slowly. He looked at Karl and gestured around. 'All this blood. If Hingis was standing close enough to your man tae cut his throat, some of that blood would have got on his clothes, maybe his face. There isna' enough on him. There's only a wee bit of blood from this stab wound.'

'A three-way fight then.' Karl looked around. 'But only two chairs at the table.'

'Three in the room, though.' Alec strode over to the one by the window. 'There's blood on it here.' He held his hand over the top of the chair's back. 'Just where you'd pick it up tae move it. And mebbe some spatter on the seat,' he added after further inspection.

'I can't see either of these two wanting to rearrange furniture after getting stabbed,' Karl remarked. 'Whoever killed them wants us to think there were only two men here. In fact, I bet these two never drew their knives at all; the killer set it up to make it look like they fell out and attacked one another.' He moved to the table. 'There's just two glasses on the table, though.'

'There's another one here.' Alec retrieved a third

glass from under the bed and held it to the light from the window. 'There's a little whiskey in it, but it's pretty clean, not smudged. That bottle of whiskey mostly went into the other two, I reckon. A quick tidy up tae make it seem like there were only two men here. If I hadna' felt there was something wrong wi' all that blood. . . .' He straightened up, suddenly alert, and hurried back to the body of Mutt Hingis. Alec touched the neck and face again, letting out a hiss of displeasure at something he saw.

'What is it?' Karl asked.

Alec whirled round, full of energy. 'Look at the blood: it's damn near wet, still. The missing man killed these two just a few minutes ago an' he can't be far away.' He passed Karl on his way through the door.

Karl saw something in Alec's face. 'You know who is it,' he said as he followed. 'You think it's York!'

Out in the corridor, they met Davy. The barman reported without being asked.

'A dude in room twelve there said he heard something like someone falling over and then someone running in the corridor, just a few minutes back.'

'You know the feller in twelve?' Alec asked urgently.

Davy shrugged. 'Some Yankee come west to sightsee.'

'Thanks.' Alec dashed to the window at the end of the corridor, the one at the back of the saloon. He peered out, grabbing a sturdy rope that hang down the outside of the wall. 'He took the fire escape rope so he didna' have to leave through the saloon.'

'Where's he gone now?' Karl asked. 'Hiding up in another saloon?'

Alec was already heading back to the stairs. 'If he's got a lick of sense he'll be quitting the town fast, hoping to get away afore someone finds the mess he made in there. Doan' let anyone in,' he added to Davy, gesturing back at room ten.

'Got it,' the barman called as the two lawmen thundered down the wooden stairs.

'Why do you think it's York?' Karl asked, as they made their way across the saloon.

'York killed everyone on that stage because he didna' want witnesses who could identify him. Mutt Hingis is – was – a known stage robber. I bet those two were York's accomplices, and York reckoned it was safer to get rid of them. I didna' see it at first, but those knife wounds were made by a larger knife than either victim was carrying.'

'York wears a bowie,' Karl recalled, following

Alec through the door onto the sidewalk.

Alec glanced up and down the street. 'We'll try Bonte's Livery first.'

'We could split up.'

Alec shook his head as he broke into a jog. 'York's too dangerous.'

They had only passed one other building when they glimpsed someone leading a horse from the livery stable further along the street. Other pedestrians on the busy sidewalk partially obscured their view. As the rider mounted, the sun caught the fair hair showing beneath a familiar hat. York turned his horse and headed away, along the street.

'Dammit!' Alec skidded to a halt, forcing Karl to swerve to avoid him. He looked around for a moment and then raced off again.

A small cluster of cowhands were just dismounting and tying their horses to the rail outside the grocery next to the saloon. Alec arrived amongst them like a whirlwind.

'I need tae borrow a mount,' he barked, glancing over the horses. 'There's a killer nearby.'

A confusion of voice asked questions as Alec seized the reins of a palomino.

'This is law work.' Karl added, drawing attention to his own badge.

'Here.' A pair of reins were pushed into his

hand. 'Take Rabbit.'

Alec vaulted into the palomino's saddle and carefully backed the horse out of the mob. He spared a glance to see that Karl was mounting a short-backed brown and then concentrated on his own, unfamiliar mount. York was riding away at a casual jog, not fast enough to draw attention to himself. Pushing his horse on, Alec followed at a slightly faster pace. Karl came alongside and the two lawmen drew their pistols. Behind them, a couple of the cowhands ran into the street to see what was happening, while the rest charged in a block along the sidewalk.

Alec felt the familiar spike of excitement and fear as he headed towards danger, but his mind was a clear as always. He gauged his pace carefully: he wanted to catch up with York, but only when the outlaw had left the busy streets of the town. Moving too fast ran the risk of drawing York's attention to him too early.

One of the young cowhands racing along the sidewalk jumped into the street. He stood still a moment and then turned back to his friends.

'Hey! That's Saul York!' He spun back and reached for the old Colt holstered at his side.

CHAPTER NINE

Alec didn't waste his breath cursing. He asked his horse to stop and the palomino obeyed so sharply that Alec swayed, missing at his first attempt to aim his gun.

'Get off the street!'

Chaos erupted at his command. Karl, surprised at the abrupt change of pace, almost passed him before halting his own mount. The young cowhand looked around wildly at Alec's order, gun drawn but not aimed anywhere in particular. A teamster yelled at his oxen, people milled on the sidewalks and one of the cowhands yelled at his friend to take cover. Up ahead, York had stopped and turned his horse, drawing as he did so.

The outlaw fired first, aiming for the young cowhand, who was the closest. The shot missed its target, who yelped with surprise. Instead, it struck a burro a few yards behind him. The shaggy brown animal staggered, braying mournfully. Alec raised his own gun to shoot, but as he did, he hesitated. The action triggered the memory of the fight against the rustlers with Sam, and his own failure. Was his gun loaded this time? Was his mistake about to put Karl's life in danger? Karl who was getting married soon ... There was a sudden iciness in his belly that he'd rarely ever felt before.

As the cowhand scrambled for cover on the sidewalk, York swung his restless horse around towards the lawmen. Alec clearly saw his pockmarked face and the cold blue eyes, aimed at him with scorn. His heart pounding, he pulled the trigger. The gun fired, the shot making the palomino shy. Reflexes took over. Alec controlled the horse with legs and his left hand, cocking his pistol with his right hand to aim again. Karl had fired too, but neither had hit at this range. Alec's head began to clear, assessing the situation in his usual calm way. He fired again and urged his dancing horse to the right. Karl moved left, controlling his snorting, prancing mount with grace. The increased distance between them meant that York could only focus on one of them at a time. York fired again as Alec moved, missing his target. Now the lawmen began to alternate shots. They were hampered by the erratic movements of their nervous horses, but time was on their side. York only had one pistol – six shots – in hand. He would run out of bullets before the two lawmen did.

'Surrender!' Alec yelled, anxious for the shooting to stop before any bystanders were hurt. 'Drop your weapon.'

York's gaze swept back and forth between the two lawmen. His expression changed to something like a sneer, then he hauled his horse around and kicked it into a gallop. Alec and Karl charged after him. The excited, sweating palomino bounded straight into a full gallop. Alec tried to steady it, but the palomino stiffened its neck and ignored his signals. Once again, Alec assessed the changing situation and a new plan formed in moments. A fierce smile appeared on his face as his warrior side rose to the challenge.

Letting the horse run as it wanted, Alec holstered his gun and reached down to unfasten the lariat tied to the saddle. York had seen that the lawmen's horses had been ridden into town already, while his own mount was fresh: he was gambling that he could outrun them in a long chase. Shooting him from the back of a galloping, gun-shy horse would be almost impossible. Alec decided to try something different.

The fast moving palomino was catching York's horse, and would soon be within range. Holding the coils in his left hand, the reins between his last fingers, he carefully shook out a loop with his right. Lariats weren't part of a cavalryman's equipment, but when he was a sergeant his platoon had been assigned to help cowhands deliver cattle to an Indian reservation. Alec and Sam had taken the chance to learn roping, and had gleefully competed with one another for a few weeks, sometimes actually roping one another for practice. It was a few years now since Alec had handled a rope, and he hoped sincerely that he hadn't lost the knack.

Every stride of the palomino brought him closer. Alec leaned forward slightly in his saddle, judging the distance carefully, almost oblivious to anything else. Making a neat, backhand swing, Alec threw for an overhead catch. The loop flew straight and dropped neatly over York's head and shoulders. Alec instantly dallied the rope around the saddle horn while halting the palomino. The horse dropped its quarters and came to a sliding halt, throwing up clouds of dust.

The rope went taut. York was hauled backwards over his horse's rump, landing in the street. Alec had assumed the golden palomino was a flashy, go-to-town horse, but it again reacted like a trained cow pony. It backed away from York, keeping the rope taut so he couldn't loosen the noose. The outlaw was too winded to struggle much anyhow. Karl caught up, his horse bouncing to a halt. He dismounted swiftly and went to disarm the trapped outlaw. Further back, the young cowhands and a few other bystanders were racing to catch up and see the excitement.

'Saul York, you're under arrest.' Alec spoke up to be heard over the whoops and laughter from the gathering crowd.

Karl cuffed York and helped him to his feet. The outlaw turned and glared at Alec.

'You got no right to do this! I ain't broke my bail!'

Alec was coiling up the rope. 'I'm arresting you for the murder of Mutt Hingis and one other person.' Now he could see the spatters of dried blood on York's shirt.

'I don't know who the hell you're talking about. I got rights, and this is harassment; my lawyer told me so after you done quizzed me about that stagecoach robbery.' York's fair skin was flushed with indignation.

'Which stagecoach robbery?' Alec asked coolly,

fastening the lariat back to the saddle.

'The Jamestown one, of course!'

'Oh, that one where you killed all the witnesses?' Alec kept the same, indifferent tone.

'Yes! You're not much of a lawman if'n you can't recall. . . .' York's furious retort trailed off as he realized what he'd said.

Alec slid down from his borrowed horse, patting the palomino's neck. He'd heard the reaction from the crowd at York's accidental confession, but kept his own satisfaction from his face. 'Och, I mind the men ye killed,' he said. 'The driver, Phil Hartington; Crewe, he was a miner; Wallis, he was a barman, and Sam Hickson. Hickson was a school-teacher. You had all four of them tied to the wheels of the stage and you killed them in cold blood. Only Hartington was armed; the rest were defence-less.'

'Hang him!' yelled a voice from the crowd.

York glared first at the angry people watching, then at Alec. 'This is ridiculous! You ain't got the right to arrest me.'

'The law says otherwise,' Alec replied. 'I'm taking you tae the county jail, where you'll be held until trial. That's the law,' he added loudly, turning to face the crowd. He made eye contact with one after another, his expression as firm as steel. Karl was holding on to York, but was standing close by in support. 'The law will take its proper course. There'll be no lynchings in my jurisdiction.'

It wasn't until the train had passed Pinewood Springs, the last stop before Lucasville, that Alec could finally relax. As Estes Park had no marshal, it had taken a little while to find somewhere he could leave Saul York securely locked up while he and Karl had finished business in the town. Karl had broken up a few groups of grumblers who'd been making threats towards York. Alec had thanked the cowhands for the loan of their horses and spoken sternly to the one who'd attempted to shoot York. After that, he'd returned to the saloon, searched the murder room thoroughly and taken notes before arranging for the bodies to be shipped back to the undertakers in Lucasville, and finally, sent a telegram to the jail.

Once on the train with their prisoner, York had complained continuously. After half an hour of being ignored, he'd resorted to foul language at increasing volume. Alec, tired and irritated, had threatened to gag York with his own bandana. The outlaw had lapsed into sullen silence, but then began fidgeting, sighing and kicking the seat in front. After putting up with bouts of this for another half hour or more, Alec had finally snapped. With Karl's help, he dragged the outlaw to the platform at the end of the car and hand-cuffed him to the iron railing. Leaving York standing outside, they informed the conductor of what they'd done, and returned to their seats.

Alec heaved a long sigh of relief. After a few moments, he said, 'I need coffee.'

'We'll be in town in half an hour.' Karl tried to console him.

'I know. Still got tae take York to the jail first, though.'

'I can do that; you go back to the office and rest,' Karl offered.

Alec shook his head. 'I want tae see this through mysel' an' the jail's no too far from the station. I'm sure I can get a cup o' coffee there, once York's locked up.'

Karl nodded. 'Let's hope Branson is on time to meet us at the station with the jail wagon.'

'If not, I'll handcuff York tae the top of the water tank an' leave him there while we wait.' Alec said. 'We won't be able to hear him from inside the station restaurant.'

Karl chuckled. 'You would, too.'

'I did once, when I was a sergeant and there was a know-it-all corporal who wouldna' be told he was riding his horse wrong.' Alec smiled at the memory, and rested his head against the back of his seat.

'Come on, I want to hear the story now,' Karl asked.

'Ask Sam; he tells it better. I just want tae enjoy some peace right now.'

Karl snorted and settled back to relax too.

They were just passing the outskirts of Lucasville when Alec and Karl went to join their prisoner. York glared sullenly, and complained about having to stand in the same position for so long.

'I'm going to see my lawyer and he'll sue the hell out of you for the way you've treated me,' York declared. 'You've disrespected me. I'm a free man and you disrespected me.'

Alec gave a humourless grin. 'You're not free. You're under arrest now and you'll be in jail in half an hour.'

'The constitution says I'm a free man!' York yelled, tugging at the handcuffs that bound him.

Alec just snorted and turned away.

The train whistled and began to slow, the cars bumping against one another as the brakeman slowed each in turn. Alec glanced up, not envying the brakeman his job, moving from the top of one moving car to the next in order to turn the braking wheels. Before joining the army, he'd spent three years working in a Chicago and North Western railyard. He'd progressed swiftly from the menial job of wiper, to actually manoeuvring the locomotives as a switchman, witnessing many injuries and two deaths during that time. As soon as he was old enough to enlist, he'd joined the cavalry, leaving the noise and grime of the railyard for horses and the open air.

As the hissing train approached the station, Alec saw a crowd of people waiting in front of the station depot.

'There's the jail wagon.' Karl pointed out the enclosed wagon amongst the haulage vehicles and the buggies waiting for passengers.

As the train drew up in clouds of steam, there was a shout and the crowd surged forward, clustering around the end of the car where the lawmen and their prisoner were.

'There's York!'

'There's the murderer!'

Alec drew his gun even before he was quite sure that people in the mob were holding shotguns and pistols. Karl was just behind his shoulder and he knew without looking that his deputy would also be checking what was happening behind them as he faced the leaders of the mob. Someone must have telegraphed the news about York from Estes Park.

'Give York to us and we'll save the cost of a trial,' shouted a man wearing a butcher's apron. Someone further back was holding up a hangman's noose. Shouts of support rippled through the mob, with a chant of 'Hang him, hang him,' forming.

Alec could see that the jail wagon was trapped on the other side of the crowd, Branson remonstrating with two men who had seized the horses' bridles. Giving York to the lynch mob would certainly be the easiest option, and, in Alec's private opinion, a justified fate for the outlaw. However, his sense of duty stiffened his shoulders.

'Hold it!' he bellowed, in his best parade ground voice. He waited, silent and still as the shouting began to die down. 'No one here is going tae be lynched today.' Now Alec spoke more quietly, forcing the crowd to hush in order to hear him. 'I'm taking Saul York here tae the prison. He'll be held there until he has his trial.'

'Not if'n that lawyer bails him out again to murder more folk!'

'Save time: hang him now.'

The chanting of 'hang him' started up again. There was a surge from the back of the crowd and the people at the front swayed closer to the rail car.

'You can't stop us, Sheriff,' bellowed a voice. Alec thought it came from a group of miners in the right of the crowd. 'There's more of us than you.'

CHAPTER TEN

Behind Alec, York was keeping up a continuous pleading for protection that grated on the sheriff's nerves.

'York ain't worth dying for, Sheriff,' called the butcher. 'You can't stop us taking him.'

Alec raised his gun sharply. 'Is he worth giving up *your* life for?' He aimed the pistol squarely at the butcher, meeting the man's eyes. 'Every man has the right tae a fair trial. It's the law and I'm here tae enforce it.' His voice was deeper, more Scottish. He didn't want to start shooting citizens, especially not to protect a man he despised, but he couldn't give in to mob rule. He made himself look as hard as granite, all the while aware of the guns pointed in his direction. 'I'm warning ye all.'

'And we're telling you to back down, Sheriff,'

came another voice. 'If you fire one shot, we can fire a half dozen back.'

'The one I fire at will be dead,' Alec replied. He kept his gaze on the butcher. 'Are you willing tae be the martyr?'

'Just shoot,' urged another voice from the group of miners.

Alec glanced out over the mob. He couldn't shoot first. Branson had his shotgun, but was too far away to help. Karl was faithfully by his side, waiting for his cue. York was sobbing and pleading, his voice like nails clawing at Alec's back. Alec's heart pounded heavily in his chest as he braced himself.

'Let me up.'

It was a woman's voice, coming urgently from the other side of the car. Alec half-turned, his eyes wide in astonishment as he recognized the voice.

'Eileen!'

Eileen Wessex climbed onto the platform from the other side of the car. She strode disdainfully past York without glancing at him, and with a muttered 'excuse me' swept in front of Karl to stand beside Alec. Recovering from his surprise, Alec was about to speak when she addressed the mob.

'Shame on you all!' she challenged. 'How can you even think of killing a good, honest man like

Sheriff Lawson? You all know how he and his deputies have risked their lives to bring in outlaws like York, here, to make this state a safer place for all of us.'

'All he's got to do is hand York over to us an' he can walk away,' shouted back one of the miners.

'Stay out of it, woman,' yelled another voice from the crowd. ' 'T'aint none of your business.'

Alec opened his mouth to speak but Eileen, her eyes blazing, got in first.

'Decent Christian virtues are the business of all of us – man or woman. The sheriff's doing the duty he swore to do.' She pointed at the butcher. 'I see you in church, Mr Stanley, most every Sunday. If you kill Sheriff Lawson here, you'll be a murderer. Can you go to church with that on your conscience?' Her accusing finger moved to another face in the crowd. 'Mr Hooper, I teach your children. How are you going to explain to Martha and Joe that you murdered a sheriff who was doing his duty and following the law?'

The butcher was studying his boots. As Alec looked into the mob, he found fewer men willing to meet his eyes.

'Are you gonna hide behind a schoolmarm's skirts?' yelled the loudest of the miners.

Alec returned a cold smile. 'I doan' have tae.'

He'd just seen a welcome sight at the far side of the railyard. Sam had just arrived at a run with Tom Clarke, the marshal, and one of his deputies. All three carried shotguns. 'If ye want tae take York, you'll be dealing with me, ma deputy here, Branson on the jail wagon there, plus the three law officers over there.' He pointed to where Sam and the others had fanned out, shotguns held at waist level.

There was some muttering as the crowd turned and looked. People on the outskirts began to drift away. Alec watched, his cold stare causing the few who looked at him to turn away. A lead weight seemed to lift from his shoulders as the mob dispersed, and he realized that York had fallen silent. A quick glance at Karl was enough for his deputy to step forward into his place and take over watching the fading mob. Alec turned to Eileen.

'Thank you. That was a brave thing you did.'

Her large, brown eyes met his. 'No, you're brave, and good.' She looked away quickly, her lovely face colouring. 'I must go.'

Alec caught her hand impulsively. 'Eileen . . . you probably saved my life just now. Saved me from shooting someone I didn't want to.'

'I'm glad,' she said softly. She met his gaze again briefly, eyes shining with tears. Slipping her hand from his, she hurried past York and swiftly let herself down the steps to the ground.

Alec watched her leave, feeling oddly wounded. Once, they'd been able to talk for hours, but now he seemed to have lost her friendship . . . or was it her trust? She had to have some regard for him, to face the mob like that, but she was always elusive when they met.

'Alec?'

Karl's voice brought him back to the present. Pushing the thought of Eileen firmly to the back of his mind, Alec set about getting Saul York to the jail.

It was the tail end of the afternoon by the time Alec returned to town. The county jail was one of his responsibilities, so after seeing York locked up, and a welcome cup of coffee, he'd spent some time inspecting the buildings and talking to the governor. Now Alec was strolling along one of the busy streets in town, trying to relax as he returned home. His route took him past the store where Lily worked, and he paused to look through the window.

She was at the counter, talking with some animation to a young man in a suit, whom Alec vaguely recognized as a junior clerk in the bank. The clerk twiddled the end of his moustache and said something that made Lily laugh heartily in a way that Alec had rarely seen her do. Alec felt a sudden stab of jealousy, and on impulse, pushed open the door and entered. Lily saw him and smiled, her face bright and lively.

'Sheriff Alec! Is so good to see you safe.'

The young man registered Alec's presence, and pushed a pair of braces a little further across the counter. 'I'll take these, Miss.' He started digging in his pocket for money.

Alec waited at a polite distance as the sale was completed, Lily ringing up the purchase on the ornate till with confidence. The bank clerk touched his hat to her, nodded to Alec, and hurried out. Lily held her hand out as Alec approached the counter.

'I heard about those people at the railway who were against you,' she said, as he took her hand. She was looking at him with genuine concern, he was sure. 'You di' a good job of bringing that bad man to jail. I don' unnerstand why they wan' kill you.'

'It was York they really wanted tae kill, but I couldna' let them do it,' Alec explained. 'I took an oath to uphold the law, an' the law says a man is innocent until proven guilty, and York has no' been found guilty by a court yet. So I couldna' let

135

them just hang him.'

Lily nodded, understanding, then smiled again. 'I am happy you are not hurt.'

'So am I.' Alec gave her delicate hand a gentle squeeze and released it.

Lily smoothed down her sleeve and composed herself neatly. 'You are looking well today.'

'Thank you,' Alec said automatically. 'Did you enjoy the drive yesterday?' he asked.

'Of course, thank you. The scenery is charming.'

'That young man, is he a friend from church?'

Lily nodded, still smiling. 'George, he works in the bank.'

The storeowner came through from the back, carrying an armful of made-to-order shirts. He frowned for a moment, before recognizing Alec. 'Good evening, Sheriff.'

'Good evening.' Alec responded. He looked at Lily. 'I'd best not take up more of your time.' With a smile for her, and a nod to the storekeeper, he left.

As he walked, Alec considered his feelings. His heart seemed to lift every time he saw Lily; that was a simple truth. She was happy in her new life, with her young friends, but she looked at him with adoration, he was sure. Would she be happy living with him on a horse ranch? It was so easy to picture her as the centre of a cosy, domestic life, keeping house and raising children. And Alec knew that that was the life he ultimately wanted for himself – he just didn't know when would be the right time.

Still occupied with thoughts of Lily, Alec opened the front door of the sheriff's building, and stopped dead on seeing his deputies lined up inside the office.

'We've been waiting for you to show up,' Karl said, picking up his hat.

'We're gonna go out and celebrate: have ourselves a real whing-ding!' Sam added.

'Celebrate?' Alec echoed.

Ethan shook his head. 'Our sheriff's been out in the sun too long. He ain't fit, remember?'

'I'm fine,' Alec protested automatically.

'Then you're good to come out and celebrate catching Saul York and getting him put back behind bars again,' Karl said. He smiled and clapped Alec on the shoulder. 'You used to know how to have fun. It's time we reminded you.'

Sam was almost bouncing up and down on the spot, an irrepressible grin on his face. 'We'll go out and stuff our faces at the best restaurant in town, then go to a saloon where we can drink and argue over a few games of poker, and dance with all the pretty girls.'

'Alec can't dance,' Ethan insisted. 'I've seen him.'

'I can so dance.' Alec defended himself with spirit.

'The Highland Fling doesn't count,' Karl said. 'Even if you were dancing it on a table.'

'Ye have no appreciation for culture.' Alec laughed, grateful for his friends. 'Let's go, then. First one under the table pays for any damages.' He turned to leave.

'That's not fair,' Ethan grumbled as they followed. 'No one can drink like a Scot.'

Alec only laughed louder.

The next few days were busy, though for Alec most of his work seemed to be writing notes, letters and paperwork, nearly all about York. The hot days in the stuffy office were frustrating. After two days of it, Alec had to get outside. After supper, he saddled Biscuit and went for a long ride by himself. Every evening after that he worked off his energy and frustration with a ride; sometimes he was alone, and sometimes he was with one of the others. In his impatience at spending his days indoors, he didn't realize that the evening rides no longer tired him.

One afternoon, Alec called on Hart, who looked

rather sulky, and grudgingly admitted that he wasn't going to stand bail for York again. Hart's evident discomfort cheered Alec in the face of the impending court appearance for York's arraignment on the Estes Park murders. York got upset when told there would be no bail. He swore at everyone in court and complained as the prison guards dragged him back to the prison wagon to return him to his cell until his trial later in the year. Alec used the excuse of inspecting saloons and brothels that wanted licences for a ride out to Lyons the next day.

The following morning, he was back at the never-ending paperwork again, mostly routine stuff that had been put off during his illness. It was getting on for mid-morning when Alec's concentration was broken by a crash as the front door of the building was flung open. Alec started, blotting the paper he was writing on as he looked up. Through the open door of his office, he saw one of the younger guards from the prison, dusty and gasping for breath as he looked around. Alec jumped to his feet, sending his chair skidding. The guard turned to the sound.

'Sheriff Lawson! York's gone and busted out of the jail!'

'What? How?' Alec demanded.

'I don't know much. Knowles sent me out pronto to tell you.'

'Goddamn it!' Alec hurled his pen at the desk, heedless of the ink spattering across his papers. 'I thought I was done wi' chasing the bastard.' Whirling around, he grabbed his hat and gunbelt, donning them as he stormed out of his office. 'What's Knowles doing now?'

'I don't rightly know. I think he was trying to figure out exactly what happened,' the guard sputtered.

The desks in the outer office were empty today: Alec's deputies were all out of town doing various jobs and there was no quick way of making contact with any of them. Alec couldn't waste time on regret. He ushered the prison guard out onto the sidewalk and followed, pausing only to lock the door. A sweaty chestnut horse was tethered loosely to a rail just outside.

'Yours?' Alec asked.

When the guard nodded, Alec swiftly unwound the reins, patting the horse on its damp neck as he moved alongside. He wanted to get to the jail as quickly as possible, and readying one of his own horses would take too long. Mounting, he turned the chestnut and urged it into a trot.

Much as he wanted to hurry, the streets were too

busy for Alec to risk galloping. He threaded through the bustle of wagons, pack animals and pedestrians as fast as he dared, using the time to consider the situation. The railyard was busy too, a locomotive steaming gently in the siding while people clutching luggage milled about. Once he'd crossed the tracks and left most of the traffic behind, he finally urged the horse into a gallop.

He'd only been riding for a few minutes before he saw another rider approaching from the direction of the jail. Alec was quick to recognize the short, study shape of Knowles, the jail's governor. Gently easing his borrowed horse to a halt, he turned its head to the wind and let it recover while he waited for the governor to reach him.

'I'm plum sorry, Sheriff.' Knowles started talking before he reached Alec. His voice jerked as he slowed to a bouncing jog before halting at Alec's side. 'I sent Patchett to let you know just as soon as I got wind of it.'

'What happened?' Alec demanded sharply. 'Have ye any idea where York's at?'

The governor flushed, his already ruddy face getting even redder. 'York used Patterson and Farlow. Talked them into helping him, then did them dirty and left them behind like the polecat he is.'

Alec remembered the names as two of the men who'd been with York in the dugout when he'd first arrested the outlaw leader.

'They were in the yard for exercise when Patterson and Farlow started up a fight with a couple of others and the rest started up just for the hell of it.' Knowles said. 'They distracted that jackleg guard while York slipped up behind him. York laid out the guard as quick as a dog can lick a dish. They got York up atop the fence and then he was supposed to help them up and over too. He's as low as a snake's belly, so he just dropped down and left them on the inside. By then, more guards were coming into the yard, so Patterson and Farlow gave up trying to climb over themselves. It took a few minutes to get the riot brought down. It weren't till my men were counting heads that they realized York weren't there. They figured he'd gone over the outer wall, so they sent someone out on foot to look for him that way. Turned out he'd got into the stable yard. While we were sorting out the riot, getting folks back behind bars and searching in the wrong direction, York beat a stableman wide open and stole himself a good horse and a pistol. No one was looking for him on horseback, so he rode out and got a good head start before anyone realized what he'd done.'

'Do ye have any idea which direction he went?' Alec asked impatiently.

Knowles nodded rapidly, relieved to have some positive information. 'He was headed this way, towards town.'

Alec thought fast. York wouldn't have risked heading into Lucasville, not after seeing a mob there demanding to lynch him a few days ago. So if he hadn't been heading into the town itself, why choose that direction? The answer came to him immediately.

'He's heading for the mountains. He'll probably quit Dereham County, but he'll stay in the mountains: he's safer there.' Alec gathered up his reins. 'Was anyone hurt bad?'

Knowles shook his head. 'No broken bones, just pretty battered and bruised. I'm real sorry 'bout this mess, Sheriff.'

'We got some talking tae do later,' Alec replied, his expression stern. 'I'll have someone send Doc Alden out to ye to see tae the men.' Turning his horse, he sent it off at a gallop.

Alec was back at the rail depot in no time. A number of people were still milling around near the stationary locomotive as he dismounted. Alec handed the horse to a labourer waiting for casual work, along with a tip, and asked him to return the

143

horse to the sheriff's office, then to send the doctor to the prison. A glance at the station clock told Alec that the waiting train was the one to Nederland, but by some good luck it was running late. Beside the gently steaming locomotive, Alec saw Webb, the owner of the Northern Colorado Railroad. He made his way over to the thick-necked businessman. Webb wore a well-made suit, but still managed to look like a labourer dressed up in someone else's clothes. His habitual smell of pipe tobacco was noticeable even over the smell of hot oil and metal as Alec got close to him.

'Webb? I need a favour,' Alec asked.

'Sure thing,' Webb said immediately. 'Whatever I can help you with, Sheriff?'

The previous summer, Alec had first stopped an attempt to drive down shares in the railroad company so it could be bought up cheaply, and then helped prevent a train from crashing. Webb subsequently regarded him with a degree of awe, which Alec felt quite unnecessary, and had given him a lifetime pass for free rides on the Northern Colorado.

Alec gestured at the train. 'I need a ride to Lyons, pronto. When's this one going?'

Webb snorted like an annoyed bull. 'It ain't.' He continued before Alec could respond. 'The damn engineer's got a hangover fit to kill an ox. I got another off sick with the runs, another quit last week and the others are all out with their locomotives. I spent the last half hour trying to find anyone who knows how to drive a locomotive but there ain't no one in town.'

CHAPTER ELEVEN

'What about you?' Alec asked the fireman, whom Webb had just been talking to.

The sandy-haired man shook his head. 'I ain't been on the footplate more than a handful of times. I don't be fixing to be an engineer for a whiles yet.'

Alec swore bitterly. 'York. . . .' He halted what he was saying, and waved impatiently for the fireman to move away.

The fireman looked at Webb, who told him to wait in the depot building. When the man was out of earshot, Alec continued.

'York's bust out of jail,' he explained, making an effort to keep his voice low. 'I'm sure he's heading tae the mountains. He's got a head start on me, but I reckoned if I could get a ride on the train, I could beat him tae Lyons an' wait for him there. Now I've tae ride hell for leather after him. I can wire Lyons and have a fresh horse waiting for me when I get there. Will ye send someone to ma office an' tell Beyer tae get Biscuit ready for me while I'm sending the wire? And doan' tell anyone about York gettin' out.'

Webb nodded, then paused, his face breaking into a broad smile. 'You don't need to do that, Sheriff. You're not an engineer, but you can drive a locomotive, can't you? You can still get to Lyons ahead of York.' He clapped Alec on the shoulder hard enough to make him stagger.

'I only ever drove the locos in the switchyard,' Alec protested automatically, turning to look at the gleaming black engine. He paused, remembering. He had driven a locomotive like this one the summer before, following an attack on it by a group of bandits. Alec had organized the train as bait in a trap, but in the fight, the engineer had been killed. Alec had successfully dealt with the outlaws and brought the train back to Lucasville, but still felt himself responsible for the engineer's death.

'You did just fine last year,' Webb told him. 'I read all about York in the newspapers. He needs a good hanging, and you've got to get after him as quick as you can before he can hurt someone else, because filth like him don't care none about other folks.'

Alec nodded: Webb was right, and all he was doing was using the train to beat York to Lyons, not setting it up as a potential battleground. 'I'll need a fireman,' he said decisively. 'I won't take any passengers, just tae keep down the risk to others. I'm no' an engineer,' he repeated. 'It'll take too long tae uncouple the cars, so I'll be wanting a brakeman too.'

'I'll get you what you need, Sheriff,' Webb promised, hurrying away.

Alec took a deep breath and then climbed into the cabin quickly to begin his checks.

Twenty minutes later, the locomotive was steaming across the prairie towards the mountains. Alec glanced quickly at the boiler water-level gauge and the boiler pressure gauge to reassure himself, then looked out of the cab at the scenery rolling swiftly past. He didn't like the noise or the smells of the machine, but he couldn't help grinning as the engine drove onwards, eating up the miles beneath its iron wheels. It was nothing like the satisfaction of a partnership with a good horse, but Alec couldn't deny the feeling of power in controlling this force of steam and speed.

'She's running pretty sweet,' said Ted, the sandy-haired fireman.

'You're keeping a good fire going,' Alec responded. 'And this part of the road's no' too challenging,' he added honestly.

The view of the prairie diminished as the track entered a cutting through one of the swells in the ground. Grassy banks rose either side and then sank away as they emerged on the other side. Ahead were the foothills of the Rockies, small and gentle compared with the jagged mountains beyond them, snow glittering on their peaks even in the summer. Alec smiled at them, his heart lifting at the sight. There was a sudden blaze of heat as Ted opened the firebox to shovel in more coal. Alec watched as he deftly spread the coal into the corners of the firebox, and they fell into conversation about life with the railroads.

The miles rolled by easily, the contours of the land changing with low hills becoming more frequent. Emerging from another cutting, Alec saw a lone rider ahead, galloping close to the track. The rider was avoiding the main trail, half a mile to the south, and had clearly taken the risk of riding through the narrow railway cutting in order to save time and distance. Alec took hold of the regulator, then paused, suddenly aware of his inexperience.

He wanted to slow the train so he could take a good look at the rider as they passed. He wasn't sure how to signal the brakeman to let him know that the train was merely slowing, not stopping, or whether the brakes on the cars were needed. There was no time to dither or ask questions: Alec pushed the regulator lever carefully, moving it just a little.

The locomotive shuddered slightly as the cars behind banged into one another. When the noise ceased and the train was running smoothly again, Alec moved the lever a little more. The clatter of uncoordinated slowing cars was repeated, and again as Alec slowed once more. By this time, they were passing the rider and Alec could see that it was definitely York. The stolen horse was dripping with sweat that had worked into white foam around the girth and where the reins touched its shoulder. A glance was enough to tell Alec that it was close to exhaustion and that York would have to slow down before long. Satisfied that he would be in Lyons with plenty of time to plan his next move, he returned his attention to the track ahead and gently pulled the regulator to start increasing speed again.

The cars jostled as they spread out in the wake of the locomotive. Alec muttered a curse as a new worry occurred to him.

'What is it?' Ted asked.

'That slowing and speeding up must ha' put strain on the couplings,' Alec said, turning to look at the car behind the tender. 'I'm hoping the train's no' broken in two.' He leaned out of the cab to look back along the length of the train.

The chestnut horse was slowing to a walk now, falling behind the train, but its saddle was empty. York was nowhere in sight. Alec swore again, louder.

'The bastard's hopped aboard!' He turned to the tender, then paused, looking at Ted. Drawing a holdout pistol from his jacket, he gave it to the young man. 'Keep yer head down. If ye see York, shoot first and ask questions later. Doan' give him a chance: he's meaner than a teased rattler. Oh, an' you're the engineer now.' With a brief grin at the fireman, he climbed onto the tender.

Alec scrambled over the coal, then swung himself carefully from the tender and across the gap to the little platform at the front of the first car. He glimpsed shining rails and wooden ties flashing past beneath him as the train swayed along, wheels rumbling. Alec didn't think about what would happen if he fell: he concentrated on getting across. With both feet safely on the wood of the platform, he drew his gun and opened the door.

Moving fast, Alec darted inside the car and behind the nearest seat, seeking cover even as he looked for York. There was no sign of the outlaw, not even a glimpse of fair hair above the other seats. The empty car, with the prairie streaming past the wide windows, seemed strange and slightly eerie. Alec heard nothing but the slightly muffled rhythm of the locomotive: no voice, no gunshots. Sliding out into the aisle, he hurried to the other end, his steps slightly uneven as the car swayed. All the time, he watched the window in the door ahead. Surely York would be puzzled by the empty train: where was he, and would he come looking for any crew?

Alec paused beside the door, looking through the window at an angle. He smiled slightly, remembering York's complaints at being handcuffed to the platform on the way back from Lyons. It seemed unlikely that the outlaw would be travelling outside this time. Moving on, Alec slipped from one car to the next. Choosing speed as the best policy, he entered the second car without pausing to look through the door first. He saw fair hair, saw York rising from a seat halfway along and turning to face him.

'Surrender!' Alec raised his gun to shoulder height as he shouted.

York started to lift his gun: Alec fired. York flinched and dropped out of sight between the high-backed seats.

'Throw out your gun an' surrender,' Alec ordered, moving forward slowly, keeping his gun ready.

'You *hurt* me!' York's indignation was fuelled by fury. 'You can't do that to me!'

'I sure can. I've got the badge tae prove it. Put down your gun!' Alec barked the order.

A wordless scream alerted Alec even before York's gun thrust out from behind the seats. He dodged, throwing himself between seats on the other side of the aisle as York fired. Two bullets zipped past, one tearing through the polished wood on the side of the seat. Pushing against the red velvet, Alec straightened himself and blind-fired a shot back down the car before peering cautiously around the seat in front. Gunsmoke hung in the air, fogging the sunlight that poured in through the windows. York was not in sight.

A shuffling noise caught Alec's attention. It was coming from York's direction, but he couldn't see what the outlaw was doing. Choosing caution, Alec emptied the spent shells from his gun and reloaded while he listened and waited to see what York was up to. He carried a dozen cartridges on his gunbelt and had dropped a dozen more into his pockets before setting out on the train. Knowles had been pretty sure that York had only taken a revolver, and hadn't been able to get any extra ammunition for it, which gave Alec an edge.

He slid out from between the seats, sacrificing cover for ease of movement. 'Come on out, York.'

There was no reply, just some muffled grunts and some scraping.

Puzzled, Alec began advancing cautiously. He was getting close to halfway along the car, almost to where York had been sitting. Alec halted again, thinking, then backed up a couple of paces. Steadying himself with his free hand on the nearest seat, he crouched and bent to look underneath the rows of seats. As he did, there was a flurry of movement at the far end. Alec jumped up as York burst into view by the door, gun raised. He'd scrambled under the seats to reach the end of the car unseen. Alec had realized too late and York had got the drop on him.

Alec threw himself sideways, twisting, as York fired. He landed sprawled across the seats and pulled his legs in, waiting for another shot. Instead there were quick footsteps and the sound of the door being opened. Alec struggled back to his feet, losing his hat as he untangled himself from the seats and back into the aisle. He saw gunsmoke in the air, but York had gone. He couldn't have got across and into the next car so fast but thumps against the end of the car confirmed Alec's suspicions: York was heading for the roof.

Sprinting back along the car, Alec hurtled through the door and grabbed the ladder. He got halfway up then slowed. Clinging to the iron rungs as the car rattled along, he raised his head over the edge cautiously. York was standing on the roof, feet planted wide apart as he swayed with the car's movement. There was a small stain on the right front of his jacket and a thin trail of blood oozing down from underneath it, onto his leg. Alec saw him aim and ducked hastily. York didn't fire. In spite of the situation, Alec smiled to himself. York was limiting his shots because he had no spare bullets. He had fired two at Alec already, so had a maximum of four left.

Alec hitched himself up so he was crouching on the ladder, his head just below the roof of the car. Making sure of the grip with his left hand, he thrust his right hand up and fired two quick shots, blind. Even as he heard York cursing, he pushed upwards, throwing himself onto the roof. Alec landed on his knees, bringing his gun up. York tried a snap shot but he was off balance and it went wild. Alec aimed precisely.

'Surrender! Drop your weapon.'

'You can't make me,' York spat.

Alec thought fast. He couldn't be sure of killing York with one shot, and if he tried to fire, York would shoot back. Being on his knees made it hard for him to dodge; he couldn't rely on York missing him with all three of his bullets. He needed a distraction. The car swayed and York tensed, fear biting his face as he recovered his balance. Alec knew what to do. He glanced to one side.

'Don't look down!' he said urgently.

York did so instinctively, seeing the ground rushing past below. He gave a yelp of fear and jerked away. As he staggered, Alec pushed himself to his feet.

'It's not fair!' York screamed, his arms out wide as he fought to keep his balance. 'You forced me to come up here.' His face was white and pinched with fear.

Alec felt a slight bump as the car rode over an uneven patch of track, but absorbed the movement easily. He aimed for the outlaw.

'Stop it. Make it st. . . .' York's angry pleadings turned to a scream as the jolt hit him. He lurched and almost landed on one knee, close to the edge of the roof.

'Don't panic,' Alec called, as the outlaw staggered about on top of the car. He started forward, but York was too far away to reach quickly.

Gripped with fear, York only thought to get away from the edge of the roof. He threw himself away from the edge and lurched erratically back towards the end of the car. 'Oh, God. Help me. Stop it. Stop!' His pleas rose to a screech. York spotted the braking wheel sticking up and lunged towards it.

Alec didn't know if York meant to hang on to it for safety, or if he planned to try and stop the train. He did know that if York tried turning it, he would more than likely cause the link between the cars to snap.

'No!' he ordered, snapping off a warning shot. 'Lie down!'

The bullet hit the metal post of the braking wheel, ricocheting off and catching York's jacket in passing. The outlaw screamed in panic, no longer in control of himself. He stumbled backwards, flailing, and tumbled over the end of the car. His scream ended suddenly. The car behind swayed as it ran over something.

Alec grimaced, but inwardly felt numb. He just

stayed where he was, riding easily on top of the car, as the wind whipped his hair. York was dead. Alec hadn't meant for him to die that way, but he'd been willing to shoot him, so did it make a difference? Alec thought of Foxtail Mary, beaten black and blue for speaking up. He remembered the guard murdered for not having the key to the strongbox, the four dead men in the back of a wagon, covered with a tarpaulin.

Taking a deep breath, Alec let it out slowly. York was dead and would never hurt anyone again. Alec knew with absolute certainty that he was doing the right thing. There was no question of retiring while he could still put things right and save families from pain. With that clarity came a sudden rush of energy. Alec turned and headed for the locomotive. There were things he needed to do.

'I guess in a way, we can thank York for saving us some work,' Sam said. 'I mean, now we know those two he killed in Estes Park were part of the Jamestown stage holdup, we don't need to go hunting for them.'

'We're don't know for certain-sure they were part of that robbery,' Ethan pointed out, dropping into his armchair with a sigh.

It was evening, and the four lawmen had fin-